Rocket from Infinity

Books for Young People
by Lester Del Rey

BY LESTER DEL REY

Rocket from Infinity

Holt, Rinehart and Winston   *New York* /

Chicago / *San Francisco*

Contents

Rocket from Infinity

It was a big day for Pete Mason. His permit to visit the Martian ruins had finally come through. He'd presented himself at the tourist section of the New Portland Space Authority, but his permit puzzled the dispatcher.

"There must be some mistake. This says the Barco ruins."

"Yes, sir."

"But you're only a kid. You can't be over seventeen."

"I'm eighteen, sir."

"All right. Eighteen. But kids aren't allowed at the ruins. It's reserved strictly for accredited scientists."

Perhaps the dispatcher was being officious or perhaps he was sincere in doing his job. It made no difference to Pete. Being barred from the ruins for whatever reason would be a terrible disappointment.

"But my permit is authentic, sir. It's signed by the Dean of the New Portland Mining College and it has the Federation stamp."

The dispatcher did not call it a forgery, but that could have been his thought as he frowned at the stamp and the signature.

"They don't want souvenir-hunting tourists out there. Valuable artifacts would be removed. Evidence would be trampled underfoot."

Pete knew all about that. Barco Village, named after Samuel Barco, the archeologist who had discovered it, was the only mark of human habitation ever found on the planet Mars. The deserted and moldering ruins of a small village uninhabited for at least a thousand years, standing alone on the planet.

By every law of logic, chance, or probability, the place should not have existed. Yet it was there, empty, mute in its ancient solitude, successfully defying the keen archeological and scientific brains that had tried to discover its secrets.

Of course, a dusty little Martian ruin didn't cause much public excitement. There was too much of a current nature going on every day on the inhabited planets and asteroids. But to the scientific world, Barco Village was important indeed. And that included Peter Mason, down from the planetoid, Juno, studying for his archeological degree at New Portland Mining College.

And now this character was making like he'd forged his own pass!

Pete was angry and he wanted to show it. But he was also smart enough to realize that a fight with the dispatcher wouldn't help him a bit.

"You could check with the Dean's office at the Mining College," he suggested.

The dispatcher glanced at his watch. "They don't open over there for two hours yet." The dispatcher's frown worked overtime as he glanced along the ramp. "In fact, the scooter may not go at all. There doesn't seem to be any passengers."

So that was it! There was still an hour to go, but the dispatcher wasn't going to send a scooter out for a single eighteen-year-old college student. It was simpler to question the pass, which he apparently had a right to do.

"But the pass is authentic," Pete protested.

The dispatcher continued to scowl at it, obviously having decided to think otherwise. But at that moment a tall, thin, middle-aged man entered the corridor and moved up the ramp. He'd evidently heard Pete's protest during his approach. He smiled and asked, "Having trouble, son?"

"Yes, sir. I have a pass to Barco Village and the dispatcher is questioning it."

"Let me see it."

With an air of casual authority, the man took the pass from the dispatcher's hand and examined it.

"Looks all right. In fact, it is all right."

13

"How do I know that signature is authentic?"

"Because I tell you it is," the man replied pleasantly. "It's my signature. I am Dr. LeRoy, Dean of the New Portland Mining College. You're new here, aren't you?"

"Yes—yes, sir," the dispatcher stammered.

"Let me commend you on your alertness. And now, if you don't mind, I'd like a scooter. This young man can ride along with me to the ruins."

The dispatcher hurried into the shed and Dr. LeRoy glanced at Pete. He had deep-set, dark eyes, and they twinkled. "Don't tell the dispatcher I issued the pass because I knew your father during my old mining days. He'd think I'm playing favorites, which of course I am . . ."

Five minutes later, seated beside Dr. LeRoy as the scooter rocketed along some three feet above the level ground, Pete said, "I want to thank you for coming to my rescue."

Dr. LeRoy didn't answer. He turned a quick, sharp gaze on Pete for a few moments, studying the not unhandsome but quietly serious face under the shock of unruly black hair.

"You don't look much like your father."

"No. Dad is heavier and stockier than I am."

"I'd say you're somewhat less of an adventurer, too. Joe Mason and I roamed the asteroid belt in old buckets that have long since been outlawed. Those were the days before things were organized. When you made a strike you protected it by force of the arms you carried with you. Your father saved my life several times. He had quite a reputation. Pirates who

14

discovered that they were facing Roaring Joe Mason often lost their predatory appetites."

Pete wished he'd been able to communicate better and tell Dr. LeRoy how proud he was of his father and how he still thrilled to the stories the old-timers told of Joe Mason.

Of course, now with the Mining Brotherhood having been created and the Planetary Federation law in effect, piracy was at a minimum and the opportunity for wild adventure greatly reduced.

"Dad mentions you often."

"He wrote me saying that you'd be down to Mars to register. That was some six months ago; then, recently, in another letter, he mentioned your strong archeological interests."

"So that was why—"

"You received the permit? Partly. It also happens that your marks qualified you—and interested students interest *me*."

The scooter flashed smoothly along across the ocher-colored expanse of the vast, dead sea floor of the planet. Uncountable eons before, these levels had been deep beneath Martian oceans.

Pete sat silent—engrossed and enthralled. Again he wished he were better skilled in the use of words. He desperately wanted to express the feeling that came over him when he thought of the majestic grandeur of the planets and the solar system; the sense of microscopic insignificance that tightened him all up when he let his mind roam farther—out into the vast unreachable spaces beyond. Why this whole system—this whole incredibly vast galaxy was but a pinpoint

15

in the infinite reaches that stretched on and on and on. Would mankind ever discover a cosmic law that would allow him to penetrate that vastness? To drive the shining ship out to where time and space had to blend and flow back into the eternal circle?

" . . . I was surprised that you didn't drop in to see me," Dr. LeRoy was saying.

"Ah—oh, I beg your pardon sir!"

"I said . . ."

"Yes, I heard you. It was just that . . . well, I didn't want to impose on a friendship between you and Dad."

"Quite commendable. What are your plans—your ambitions?"

"I want to be the best archeologist in the System."

"Very clearly put. But why archeology? Why not mining?"

"It seems to me the natural history of the planets is very important. And so far as mining is concerned—well, it's all pretty much been done. In the main, it's routinized."

"There are a few rugged individualists left in the Belt," Dr. LeRoy said.

"Yes, but there are so many exciting archeological discoveries waiting to be studied. I want to be a part of the future."

The ghost of a smile played on Dr. LeRoy's lips as he lifted the scooter a few feet to top a rise. "And I am sure you will be."

"I'll certainly try."

"Do you have any theories on the mystery of Barco Village?"

"I haven't any of my own, but I know most of the theories that have been put forward. One that I like claims some advanced civilization on one of the Outer Planets ran into trouble and was destroyed after its scientists had developed the technology to cross to the Inner Planets nearer the sun. If that had happened, they could have left the village stranded. I think it's certainly safe to say the inhabitants came from another planet. They had to. There's ample proof that they didn't originate on Mars."

"The logic is sound. But what about the evidence of two separate races in the same village? One was of about average size, but the others could not have been more than three feet tall."

"I'd say the superior race, whoever they were, brought slaves with them."

"That idea is accepted by some, rejected by others."

Less self-conscious now that the discussion had embraced his favorite subject, Pete said, "I'd say the big mystery is why, after establishing the village and living there for at least a thousand years, the race left the planet."

"Perhaps they were abducted by a superior race and became slaves themselves," Dr. LeRoy said.

"And what did they do with their dead during the thousand years? Where was their burial ground? Our only knowledge of what they looked like comes from the pictures they left behind on the walls."

"The bodies of the dead could have been totally destroyed. That could have been a part of their funeral process. I'd say the most mystifying part of the riddle is the contrast."

"The contrast, sir?"

"Accepting as fact, their arrival by spaceship, we must also accord them great scientific and technological ability. Yet the village is quite primitive. It indicates the presence of a backward people."

"Also," Pete said, warming to the subject, "how could a race with a pioneering spirit great enough to bring them through the void, be content to remain static in Barco Village for a thousand years? They should certainly have developed the planet's facilities and expanded their foothold or they should have left."

"I have a theory of my own," Dr. LeRoy said, "that is tenable in that it answers every question ever brought up concerning the ruin."

Pete's eyes widened. "Then you should certainly write a paper on it."

Dr. LeRoy lifted the scooter a hundred feet in the air to recheck his bearings. From that height Pete could see what had to be the celebrated ruin called Barco Village.

He pointed. "There it is!" he cried. "There it is!"

Dr. LeRoy smiled again, fully understanding Pete's excitement. To an archeological student, first sight of legendary Barco Village was a thrill indeed.

"We'll be there in five minutes."

A great deal of Pete's poise vanished, his excitement overriding it. "I can hardly wait!"

Then a female voice cut in on the open radio circuit.

"Dr. LeRoy . . ."

"Yes, Dora." He glanced at Pete. "My secretary."

There was a tone of quiet urgency in the voice as she said, "May I speak with you privately?"

"Of course."

Dr. LeRoy took a cord and earpiece from his pocket and made the attachments.

"Yes, Dora. I'm ready."

He had slowed the scooter down somewhat, and Pete watched the ruins grow slowly larger. He could not help hearing one end of the conversation.

"When did the message come?" Then, "I see . . . Very well. We'll return immediately."

Pete's heart fell as Dr. LeRoy took the earpiece away and put the cord back into his pocket. "An emergency, sir?"

"I'm afraid so, Pete. Dora checked the Space Authority and learned that you were with me. The emergency involves you."

Pete could think of only one possibility. His eyes widened in alarm.

"Dad's not . . .?"

"He's been in an accident, son. The first details were sketchy, but it's serious. You must go home immediately."

Pete was stunned. Dad hurt! How badly? What kind of an accident? These questions shot through his mind, but he was afraid to ask them. At the moment it seemed better to wait and hope.

He sat mute as Dr. LeRoy banked the scooter and reversed direction. He forgot Barco Village, his near-arrival, his *almost* exploration of the fabulous ruin.

His mind coming slowly out of the shock, he wondered again how bad it was. Would Dad die?

As the scooter kited back toward New Portland, he tried to visualize what life would be like without his bluff, wonderful, forthright father.

19

The visualization was a failure.

There was a silence for a time, then Dr. LeRoy, a man with great experience at facing emergencies, spoke as calmly and quietly as though he were commenting on the weather.

"I'll pre-empt emergency passage on a Federation ship. Their routings are by far the most frequent."

"Thank you, sir. The Federation ships are the fastest, too."

"Buck up, son. Joe is tough and durable and he's still alive. I'm sure everything will be all right. . . ."

It was toward Juno that the sleek black and silver Federation spacer set its hurtling course and the trip would take seven full days; a trip that would take the ship a few million miles out of its way, but regulations could be stretched at times.

Although Pete Mason was thoroughly familiar with the processes involved, the romanticism in his nature caused him at times to react with wonder. A tiny dot of metal called a spaceship finding with unerring accuracy one small asteroid out of 250 million others. Of course, there were far more asteroids than that out in

21

the vast reaches called the "void"; the total number could only be roughly estimated. But that figure roughly totaled the number that were large enough to be mined; a half-mile or more in diameter.

Juno was 127 miles in diameter, a huge world when compared to the average asteroid, and returning for Pete was somewhat like going back into the cold and darkness, because it got only about twenty-five percent of the light and heat the sun delivered on Mars.

But the asteroids were his home. He'd been born in the spaces of the Belt on the battered old *Windjammer*. An eight-jet space-freighter, it was of a slow, lumbering duck-like class, but ideally suited for mining, in that its hold was shaped like the belly of a bloated whale. The *Windjammer's* class could carry enough high-grade ore to make prospecting a potentially profitable operation.

Pete did not remember his mother. She'd died a year after he was born, his father turning resolutely from his grief in the interests of the son his lovely young wife had left him.

Stubbornly refusing to allow a separation, Joe Mason had spurned the offers of Earthside relatives and had taken on a nurse—sixth generation Martian—ancient and wrinkled, but marvelously wise and gentle, who was a mother to Pete until she, too, passed on during his eighth year.

From that time on he and his father had been very close. Side by side they combed the Belt for minerals and led the wild, free life of the space miner.

And Pete knew the Belt as his home. This identifying term actually meant the comparatively small

22

cluster of asteroids that one ship was capable of covering. The Belts, in reality, covered the vast patterns that the asteroids—the sands on the deserts of space—formed. Although they were incredibly wide and unchartable in their entirety, there were predictable patterns in the formation and movements of the clusters that made up the belts. It was on these movements and patterns that the space miners depended in their operations.

But Joe Mason had vowed his son would never become an "ignorant rock-crusher." Education was the ticket and Pete was going to get it till it ran out his ears!

So when Pete, at twelve, had absorbed the Elementaries, the fundamental education that was channeled by radio to asteroid children, his father enrolled him in a specialized preparatory school on Parma, the largest of the planetoids in the Belt. It was there that Pete decided on archeology as a profession, thus making a course at New Portland imperative.

But now that phase of his education had been cut short by tragedy, and he was on his way back to Juno, the Mason home base.

The Federation ship *Harlem* was a comfortable, even an exciting spacer to ride, but Pete still counted the hours of passage. Even more so because of the disquieting news he'd received from Juno. His father had been injured when a load of shale was dumped on him, and very lucky because he was in not too bad shape. But shale just didn't get dumped on people. Mining didn't work that way. The implication was sinister.

23

Pete talked to his father over radiophone his second day out—after he'd gotten the radiographed word. But the conversation hadn't been reassuring. In fact, it had been most frustrating because his father had not explained anything and brushed off Pete's questions. His gravel-voiced greeting was reassuring.

"Pete! Will you get the thunder back here and start running things? These idiots won't let me out of bed."

"Dad. That load of shale—"

"The blasted crew is deserting."

"But—"

The radio man, Paul Ames, was sitting by in the cabin. He was a clean-cut earthman fresh out of Federated Space Communication School and he and Pete had gotten on well. Ames, interested and friendly, said, "He sounds in pretty good shape."

The voice out of space crackled over the receiver. "Who's that loud-mouth cutting in? Speak up, Pete?"

"I'm here, Dad. Are you sure you're as well as you claim?"

"Who'd you say it was?"

"Paul Ames. The radio man. A friend of mine."

"All right, if he's a friend, tell him to get a little speed out of that Federated pickle jar. You're needed here. I've got five claims staked, and I just got word that the *Snapdragon* is nosing around in that area."

"You mean Rachel Barry's ship?"

"Yes, Rachel Barry's ship," Joe Mason mimicked angrily. "What other *Snapdragon* prowls the Belt trying to steal from honest miners?"

"Somebody ought to do something about those pirates!"

24

"I'll blamed well do something when I get out of this plaster box they put me in! I'll spread that flying junk yard all over the Belt. But in the meantime, you get back here and hold the line!"

"I'm coming as fast as I can, Dad. Now you take it easy and get plenty of rest—hear me?"

"Quit wasting words! I don't have to pay space-phone rates to get advice like that. You just get here!"

After the disconnect, Pete dropped weakly into a chair.

There was a lull in reception, and Paul Ames had some time to bat the breeze. "That stuff about pirating —I thought the Federation Authority arm had things under control out there."

Pete settled back into his chair and extended his long legs. He felt comfortable with Paul Ames and enjoyed talking with him.

"The main force against lawlessness is the Mining Brotherhood, with the Federation backing it up."

Paul Ames frowned thoughtfully. "That's strange. The books I read called that outfit a vigilante organization. It said they had a way of taking the law into their own hands. The Federation didn't care too much for them."

"You must have read an old book. They were a vigilante group in the beginning and they were pretty rough. I know, because my father is one of them. There was no law and order in the Belt then, and each man had to protect his own."

"An operation like that usually ends up with a group of strong men shouldering out the weak."

"Not necessarily. Of course, in the beginning it took

25

a strong man to protect his own claim. That changed, though. The Mining Brotherhood isn't against anybody prospecting the Belt and staking claims."

"What are they against?"

"Piracy. Claim jumping. They can come in swinging if it's necessary, but as I said, things have changed. They don't make and enforce their own law. Sometimes they hold the line until the Federation can get into action, but they're no lynch mob."

"From what I've heard—"

"Of course," Pete added quickly, "it's no tea party we're running out there. Some tough characters have come and gone in space mining and some of those left are still tough enough to defend their own property."

"So they're against piracy."

"They fight bleeding, too."

"What does that mean?"

"It's not actually against the law, but it's against *our* law. It means taking the top off a strike—skimming off pure ore when it's found and leaving deposits that take work and effort to get out."

"It would seem to me that the asteroids ought to be loaded with ore you could lift off with no work."

"That's not necessarily true. There are limits to everything. The Brotherhood doesn't believe in grubbing poor ore, and resents lazy operators who don't like to use machinery and leave rich deposits because mining them would take a little work. We call that *bleeding*. It's not illegal or criminal. You might call it a *gray* area of conduct. Not exactly black."

But what was that about a pirate ship your father called the *Snapdragon*? You said it belonged to a

Rachel Barry. Are there female pirates in the Belt?"

"Rachel Barry is a specialized case. A real individualist. In a way, you have to admire her."

"How can you admire a pirate?"

"She can hardly be called that. But she's got a brother-in-law, Homer, who's a different proposition. Rachel married Jack Barry, a pretty good man. They had three daughters. Then Jack Barry died a couple of years ago, and everybody expected Rachel to move to one of the planets and go on raising her family. But she didn't. She's carrying on out in the Belt. They've even got a cat they made a little space suit for. But the miners weren't able to laugh Rachel off the beltways."

"She sounds interesting."

"She is. I've never met her, but they say she's a pretty fiery old gal. She claims she's got as much right there as anybody else. She embarrassed the miners, I think—a woman doing a man's work. And I guess she does—well, let's say she's in the gray area. And there is her brother-in-law, Homer."

"She *must* be quite an embarrassment to the Brotherhood," Paul Ames said. "Pushing a woman out—a woman raising a family—isn't good public relations."

"I'll grant you that. But we can't have our claims raided, either."

Paul Ames yawned, his interest in the Belt miners and their problems beginning to wane. "How do you think your father's accident will affect your career? You said you were studying to be an archeologist."

"I don't know," Pete said gloomily. "My first obligation is to Dad, of course. If he is permanently laid up, I won't be going back to school."

"Were you on a scholarship?"

"No. That's another thing. My marks weren't quite high enough, so there's the money to be considered."

"I'm sure it will work out all right," Paul Ames sympathized.

"Of course. At the worst, being an asteroid belt miner is a good life. We work hard, but there's always the chance of the big strike. Hit the right rock and you can settle down planetside and live like an industrialist."

Paul Ames eyed his friend keenly. "But you wouldn't do that, would you?"

"No," Pete answered slowly. "I guess I wouldn't."

"And you wouldn't get a really big thrill out of striking it rich."

"It would—"

"It would give you a chance to become an archeologist."

Before Pete could answer, the Federated Fleet call letters came over the speaker. "The twenty-four-hour newscast from home," Paul said, coming erect in his chair. He adjusted the dials on the board in front of him.

Pete watched his new-found friend. Home to Paul meant Earth. Conversely, to Pete, Earth meant a faraway planet, important because it was the location of authority for the whole System. The Planetary League had its seat on Earth. The Federation authorities, all the various branches, had primary location on the lush green planet where living conditions were ideal for the human animal and where all space science had been born.

Still, Pete had no great urge to go there. He lived and moved and had his being in the Belt, with Mars as the planet from which he and his kind drew support and maintenance.

Earth, so far as he was concerned, might be an interesting place to visit. But who would want to live there?

"It's about time," Joe Mason snorted. "What did you have to do? Get out and push that Federated bucket of bolts?"

"We came in pretty fast, Dad. And I had to get here to Parma from Juno, where the ship dropped me. I borrowed a monocar from Joe Burke at the supply depot."

"Least he could do," Joe grumbled. "And now that you're here, I've got a job for you. There's a Brotherhood meeting tonight. It's an important one. You've got to represent us at that meeting."

The thought of the *Windjammer* set down beside the rambling structure the Masons called home there on the planetoid Juno had warmed Pete's heart as he spiraled down from the *Harlem*. Someday, when the Masons found time, they planned to melt an underground dwelling into the solid rock of Juno. But with the pair of them occupied with more important things, the slab-aluminum prefab would have to do—as it had done for the previous dozen years—ever since the Masons had settled into a permanent base.

Pete had hurried through the house and into his father's bedroom where he'd been hit by mixed reactions. The sight of the older man trussed up in white plaster like a cocoon had dismayed him. But the energetically snorted greeting had been most encouraging. Joe Mason was not about to join the dead.

Seated near the bed was another familiar figure, a grizzled old spaceman who looked to be a hundred and ten years old but who was in truth a mere eighty-seven. His face was like seamed leather and was fashioned into a look of permanent pessimism.

He eyed Pete sourly and said, "Betcha they didn't feed you enough on that scow to keep your stomach off your backbone." His eternal sourness had created the old man's image and his compulsive use of the first word he'd uttered had given him a name. He was Betcha Jones. He had no other identification.

Pete smiled affectionately as Betcha shifted his head slightly and put a head of tobacco juice dead center into the spittoon beside the bed.

"You should eat a meal on one of those Federation

31

ships, Betcha. You'd change your tune."

After his initial outburst, Joe Mason had lain motionless, his clear, eternally narrowed eyes looking deep into his son's face. The older man's expression did not change, but his look was still eloquent. It reflected his love for the only precious thing he had left—his son.

"You all right, boy?"

"I'm fine, Dad. But what about you?"

"Look, son, I'm too tough an old warhorse to—"

"Dad, I want the truth. That load of shale—"

The old man scowled. "I can't prove anything. I *was* in a kind of dangerous spot. I was checking some old diggings out in the cluster to see if they'd been really worked or just bled—skimmed off."

"You were alone?"

"Uh-huh. And the load of shale I got just might have shaken loose from above, but—"

He stopped, still scowling.

"But what?"

"I climbed out on my own power but I was a little dizzy. I'll swear I saw a ship pulling away, but no, I can't swear it. It might have been an asteroid rolling out of position in the cluster."

"Well, you're still alive. I guess we'll rate that as our good luck—and call it an accident for want of proof."

The frown was gone now. "Not too disappointed at having to come back?"

Pete sat down on the edge of the bed and made a fake pass at his father's bearded jaw. "Cut out that kind of talk. It's great to be here. I was getting bored at school."

Joe Mason accepted Pete's white lie, but was not fooled by it. "Won't be long," he rumbled. "I'll be on my feet in a couple of weeks—"

"Want to bet?" Betcha cut in.

"Shut up, you old space rat. I said two weeks. Pete can call it a vacation. We'll operate light. You can carry me into the *Windjammer* and we'll just cruise around and protect our interests."

"What's this about a Brotherhood meeting you want me to attend?"

"Oh, that—It's important because there's been too much piracy going on lately. We've got to do something about it."

"The Federation patrols—"

"Those bureaucrats? They're so wound up in their own red tape they could watch a bleeder stripping a mine and not make a move until they radiophoned Earth and got a go-signal from those chairwarmers down there. In the meantime, we're being robbed blind."

The Federation men, Pete fully realized, weren't as bad as his father painted them. They were just on uncertain ground because, while the Federation backed the Brotherhood in spirit, there were no clear-cut laws to guide the patrol ships. They were authorized to make arrests on the basis of certain specific complaints of a criminal nature. But moving on their own discretion could lead to all sorts of complications.

"All right, Dad. I'll take in the meeting and report back to you."

"You do that, son. And if any action is brought up to move against pirates, you vote aye, understand?"

33

"Sure, Dad. I'm going to take a shower now. And maybe I will have a bite to eat."

"You could o' taken your shower on the *Harlem*," Betcha grumbled, "and used their water instead of ours. The tanks are low."

"Okay. I'll wash my face instead. How many crewmen are left?"

"Two," Joe Mason said. "The other six went off to other jobs."

"Two of 'em still squatting in the crew quarters because they're too lazy to hunt for work," Betcha growled.

Pete turned to leave the bedroom, shaking his head in good-natured frustration. It seemed the crew members couldn't get a unanimous vote of confidence whatever they did.

He washed and ate a cold snack and got ready for the meeting.

The Mining Brotherhood had established a headquarters on Parma as being the largest centrally located planetoid in that section of the Belt. A supply base was also located on Parma and there a man could stop off and relax in the bars and get a little of the space dust out of his throat. This helped to make for good attendance at the meetings. A lot of the Brotherhood members could usually be found in Parma anyhow.

Pete jetted over in his own monocar, arriving to find a hundred-odd of the three-hundred-man membership present.

They were of a pattern, these hardy men who

34

roamed the beltways in one of the last gestures against technological regimentation left to mankind. The belt miners all aged quickly—up to a point. Thus, they all wore the badge of their calling, a tough, seamed, leathery face.

But beyond a certain point, they appeared to age not at all. There was something about the life, for all its hardships, that promoted longevity. It also seemed to promote frankness and a direct manner, for there was little guile in any of them.

Pete answered questions from friends as to his father's condition and then found a seat near the rostrum where Jerry Sells, the President of the Brotherhood took over and banged down a gavel held in a massive, weather-beaten hand.

"I now call this here meeting to order," he bellowed.

There was a gradual cessation of conversational overtone, but it was too gradual to suit Jerry. He let loose a second bellow.

"All right! Shut up, you rock busters!"

This brought silence and Jerry Sells glowered at them in triumph.

"You got something important to say, Jerry—then say it," demanded a voice.

"It's plenty important. Something's got to be done about them pirates!"

A cheer went up. Someone yelled, "Throw 'em out of the Belt!"

"Shut up!" Jerry Sells roared. "Now I want a show of hands. How many of you have had claims jumped lately?"

A dozen hands went up, including one raised by a

man, nicknamed Blaney, whose other arm was in a sling. "Me," Blaney called out, "I got jumped by three pirates in an old Class Four freighter. A little quarter-mile rock that was dripping nugget gold. When I tried to fight 'em they winged me, and I was lucky to get away that easy."

"What about the Federation patrol ships?" someone asked.

"Sure! I located one and called it in. They made me come aboard, and we spent an hour signing forms. Then when we got to my claim, those rats were gone. So darned if we didn't sign a lot more forms. They said they'd let me know."

A burly miner yelled indignantly. "It was claim jumping. There's laws about that."

"There's no law but our own," another miner cried out. "We'd better start enforcing it."

"Now hold everything," Jerry Sells bellowed. "This here meeting's getting out of order. You all know it's not legal to carry guns in the Belt."

"Whose side are you on?" the wounded man demanded.

A huge, bearded miner stood up near the rostrum and thus commanded a certain amount of attention. "I got a complaint I want something done about."

"What's that, Dave?" Jerry Sells asked.

"Hey! What about me?" Blaney demanded.

"You already been heard," Jerry said. "Go on, Dave. You got the floor."

"Fine meeting this is," Blaney growled as he sat down.

"I want something done about that crazy Barry

36

woman—Rachel Barry. She walked in on one of my claims—Rachel Barry and her daughter—and they bled me out of a ton of high-grade stuff and pulled out. I want something done about her. You can't punch a dame in the jaw!"

Someone called out, "Did you have the claim filed, Dave?"

Dave Wilson grumbled, "Well, no. I was just fixing to, though."

It was about what everyone expected. It was generally known that Dave Wilson liked the settlement bars better than the hard work on the asteroids.

There was a general laugh and somebody yelled, "Why don't you marry her, Dave?"

A man with a small sense of humor, he stared at the questioner. "Are you crazy? Marry a dame with kids like she's got? That teen-age girl of hers is a rough package."

A howl of mirth went up, diluting some of the anger that had charged the air of the meeting hall.

Pete Mason, enjoying the meeting but taking no part in it, laughed with the rest and wondered when the meeting would get down to some constructive work.

Then the door at the rear of the hall opened and Pete turned with the rest and saw three people enter.

"Well, speak of the devil," Jerry Sells said. "Or at least, the devil's wife. What do you want here, Rachel?"

The older woman in the trio was a plump, motherly looking person with mild blue eyes and an open, disarming manner. "Why, Jerry Sells," she accused. "That's a terrible thing to say about a body."

Pete was surprised. With the distances involved and his having been away at school, his never having seen Rachel Barry before was not extraordinary. But he'd hardly expected a plump motherly type. Observing her for the first time, he wasn't sure what he had expected, not knowing quite what a fire-eater would look like.

The miner called Dave was scowling ferociously. "You got a nerve, Rachel. Coming here after all the ore you been stealing from the boys."

"Stealing!" Rachel Barry stared in what appeared to be honest amazement. "I only take what I find lying loose on the asteroids."

"Sure! Ore somebody else loosens."

"But there's plenty to go around. And I've got a family to raise."

"And we're paying the bill," someone yelled.

"That's a mean thing to say," Rachel Barry protested. "You're all strong men. I'm only a weak woman. I haven't got the strength to mine ore the way you do!"

"You got me crying in my beard," a miner hooted. "Let's take up a collection for her."

Pete was only half listening. His attention was on the girl who stood between her mother and the broad-shouldered, bush-bearded man who had come in with them. This was Jane, Rachel Barry's oldest daughter.

Pete knew Jane Barry by sight. They'd been at school on Parma at the same time—before Pete went off to higher classes on Mars. But he'd never been

38

particularly attracted to her. In fact, quite the opposite. He'd seen her as bold and brassy and not his idea of what a well-bred girl should be.

They'd exchanged casual hellos, and it had not been snobbishness on Pete's part because Jane had shown no inclination to cultivate his friendship either.

So that was how it had stood—two people whose personalities didn't seem to mesh.

The man who had accompanied the two women hung back. He was frowning and seemed either worried or embarrassed.

As Jerry Sells pounded his gavel for order, the wounded miner came to his feet and pointed to the trio. "Hey!" he yelled. "I wanna—"

Jerry Sells had straightened his walking-beam shoulders and taken a deep breath. "*Shut up!*" he bellowed in a voice that shook the walls.

The wounded man dropped into his seat as though he'd been hit on the top of the head. "I was only gonna tell you . . ."

"We'll have some order in this meeting or I'll start cracking some heads. Now, Rachel—why did you come here? This is a Brotherhood meeting. You don't belong to the Brotherhood, so you don't belong here."

"But I want to join," Rachel Barry said brightly.

"She wants to join!" a member groaned. "She steals our ore and then comes in and wants to be one of us."

Another called, "Wouldn't you rather we'd all give you orbit charts on our best claims, Rachel?"

"That's not fair!" Rachel Barry protested.

It was at this point that the real excitement started.

39

Jane Barry, her eyes flashing anger, had just stepped forward in her mother's defense. "You're all mean and greedy and heartless," she cried. "I wouldn't *let* my mother join your Brotherhood—"

She was interrupted by the wounded Blaney who had been sulking over the injustices done him. His indignation rekindled, he came resolutely to his feet and pointed again.

"I got a complaint, blast it! That bushy-face there is one of the three bleeders that stole my ore!"

The reaction of the men was instantaneous.

A sudden question came into Pete's mind. The man that the complaining Blaney pointed to was Homer Deeds. Could he also have been responsible for the load of shale dropped on Pete's father? An ugly roar went up and chairs were tipped over. Nearby miners moved toward the male member of the Barry trio and he took a slow, backward step.

Without thinking, Pete was up and out of his chair. The danger here was potent. The mood of the miners was such that violence could flare instantly. In fact it *was* flaring, and Pete's instincts threw him into action.

He leaped forward and grabbed the bearded man by the arm, putting himself in the way of the advancing miners. His quick movement threw them slightly off-balance and they hesitated.

"Out! Quick!" Pete snapped. He pushed the man toward the door.

Rachel Barry, not able to react quickly, had looked around, confused, and been pushed down into a chair. Thus, she was out of harm's way.

But Jane had turned and was on the other side of

the bearded man, helping Pete push him toward the door.

"Hurry, Uncle Homer!"

They went through the door and Pete slammed it behind him and turned the key that had been left in the lock when the meeting opened.

They were in the anteroom now. The anteroom was a feature of practically all buildings in the Belt, public or private; the place where magnetic boots, an absolute requirement for outdoor movement, were left; they resembled rubbers used on the bigger planets during rainy weather.

"Grab a pair!" Pete directed as he dived toward the pile.

The man Jane had called Uncle Homer seized a pair of the boots and started toward the door.

"No," Pete said. "Put them on. We'll have time. It's worth it."

He picked up a pair and handed them to Jane, but she pushed them away, her eyes snapping. "I'll get my own, thank you!"

Pete's anger flared. "All right, you little spitfire. But do it! Don't just stand there. Those men mean business."

Someone hit the door now and Pete knew the next battering effort would be greater and the door would soon give. He regretted that the magnetic unit switch was not in the anteroom. Had that been the case he could have switched it off and degravitized the hall, leaving the miners to flounder helplessly.

"All right," he said, "let's go!"

Uncle Homer was already pulling his boots toward

the outer door. It was like a man walking in deep mud, with the double pull of the boots and the hall's gravity unit.

Jane was straining at her boots, lifting them with great difficulty. Pete seized her arm to help. Angrily, she shook it off.

"All right," he snapped. "Stay here, then. They won't hurt you or your mother."

Jane reversed quickly. "No! I want to go too. Please help me."

Pulling his extra burden toward the already opened door, Pete pushed Jane through after Uncle Homer, who had helped no one but himself. Instantly the double gravity pressure abated and the three were able to run along the surface of the asteroid against the adjusted gravity pull of the boots.

"My car's right over there. Hurry. It will carry three in an emergency."

The door had smashed open inside, and now Pete's wisdom in stopping to don the boots became apparent.

The pursuing miners didn't take the time. They snatched up boots in both hands and rushed through the outer door. The result would have been funny if the situation hadn't been so fraught with ugly danger.

A skilled acrobat could carry a pair of boots on a low-gravity surface and do very well, but it took practice that the miners didn't have. The trick of moving against a gravity that pushed downward from their hands, rather than pulling against the asteroid surface from their feet, was too much for most of them. Fine balancing abilities lacking, their hands and feet changed places and the dozen or so who had emerged presented the grotesque picture of a pursuit group walking on their hands.

Thus, pursued only by the yells of rage from the comparatively helpless miners, Pete was able to cram his companions into his monocar and take off in safety.

He lifted the car some hundred feet and arced around until he found the beep and then straightened away on the three-second beam.

"Where are we going?" Jane Barry asked.

"I'm pointed toward Juno, but we can't go too far with this load. Where is your ship?"

"We're cabled down on Pallas, but I can't leave Parma now. I've got to wait for Mother."

The little black-haired vixen was beginning to really annoy Pete. "Then why didn't you stay with her?"

"You said they wouldn't hurt her—and they won't."

"Of course they won't. They'll see that she gets back to her ship, too."

In truth—as Pete well knew—the miners of the Brotherhood had a sort of grudging regard for Rachel Barry. While rough and uncultured, they were nonetheless chivalrous. Their complaints against Rachel were mainly from frustration. They saw her as a zany addlepate more than an enemy; an annoyance more than a menace.

The three were packed in like sardines and now Uncle Homer writhed and spoke for the first time. "You can let me out here. It's safe now. I'll make my own way."

Pete made no objection as he started to lower the monocar. He didn't like the man and was embarrassed at even appearing to be on his side.

"Where will you go, Uncle Homer?" Jane asked. There was concern in her voice.

He mumbled something about having friends, thus not really answering her question, and then climbed out of the monocar and moved off into the darkness without a word of thanks.

"The grateful type," Pete murmured with sarcasm he couldn't hide.

Jane turned on him as he again lifted the car into the black space above. "You want thanks? All right. I'll thank you for him. *Thanks.*"

"I wasn't asking for gratitude."

"Then what *were* you asking for?"

"Nothing. Absolutely nothing. The next time I'll let them take your uncle out and toss him into space."

"And they'd do it, too. They'd throw an innocent man off an asteroid without giving him a chance to say a word in his own defense."

Scowling, Pete pushed angrily at the headpiece of his oxygen unit. It was attached to the supply belt, a unit all Belt people wore as an article of clothing, attaching the headpiece whenever they stepped out of pressurized areas. The unit was so constructed that the headpiece was pulled down to the belt on a light spring when not in use. But the spring on Pete's unit was out of adjustment and the headpiece kept pushing back up toward his face, giving him a somewhat undignified appearance.

"Milt Blaney identified him as one of the men who robbed and shot him, didn't he?"

44

"He *said* Uncle Homer was one of them. But how could he be sure? Is that enough evidence to destroy a man?"

"I'm not siding with the miners. I'm not defending them. I saved your uncle from them, didn't I?"

"Good lord! Do you want a medal?"

Pete realized he'd never before known the meaning of pure frustration. How did you argue with a stubborn creature like Jane Barry? The headpiece came up and pushed against his mouth. He jerked it down.

"Why don't you get that thing fixed? You look ridiculous pushing it away all the time."

"We were talking about your Uncle Homer, not about my oxygen unit. I've heard a few things about him."

"You mean you've heard things about the Barrys. Everybody talks about us."

"We were talking—"

"About the Barrys," Jane went on furiously. "You've no doubt heard things about Mother and me and my sisters. Tell me—what have you heard about my little sister, Colleen? She's eight years old. Does she go around jumping claims, too?"

"You're—you're impossible!" Pete muttered through gritted teeth.

Jane's glowing eyes reflected pleasure in the light from the monocar's radar screen. She enjoyed the helpless anger she'd produced in Pete.

"Your headpiece is hitting you in the face again," she said sweetly.

Pete jammed the pesky thing back into its tube and when he spoke again it was with grim relief. Gauging

45

himself by the Juno blip on the screen, he'd angled across to nearby Pallas and was finally happy to announce, "There's the *Snapdragon*," and almost added: I hope it collapses on the next take-off. Then he realized he was being childish and swiftly repaired his manners. "I'll drop you by the port."

"Thank you," Jane said icily.

And on that note, they parted, Pete breathing a deep sigh of relief as he lifted the monocar off Pallas and headed for home. The night had held more excitement than he cared for. He was an orderly, reasonable person, he told himself stoutly, and he liked orderly procedures and reasonable people.

Therefore, he would send Betcha Jones to the next Brotherhood meeting.

And he'd definitely avoid meeting Jane Barry again.

The next morning Pete slept late. His knowing this was more instinctive than anything else as there were few visible signs to indicate time in the Belt. The light from the sun was of a fairly steady density everywhere on the sunless sides of the largest planetoids. This density would have been considered little more than twilight by the natives of the great inner planets, because the reflective surfaces in the Belt were skimpy and broken—about the same as the Earth's sun, standing a foot or so above the horizon.

Chronometers measured the passing hours and days, of course, but Pete knew it was late on the basis that Belt people calculated their days and nights—by merely glancing out the heavy quartz window and thus giving his instincts some scant material to work with.

He got out of bed and indulged in the luxury of a shower, visualizing Betcha's objections, had he known. Betcha considered such ridiculous personal sanitation as completely unnecessary. "Nonsense kids learn at them fancy schools," he'd once snorted.

After a rubdown, Pete donned his heat unit, another of the personal items vitally necessary in the Belt. This consisted of a light garment worn next to the skin, a tight-fitting union suit that was battery-heated into a thermal shield against the steady zero-minus-one-hundred-degree temperature outside the enclosures. Maximum convenience was achieved by almost instantaneous heating at the simple snap of a switch. Also, the suit had specially constructed collars and cuffs that threw out quick heat to protect otherwise exposed surfaces, although helmets and gloves were not scorned.

Dressed for the day, Pete passed the kitchen where Betcha had left his breakfast on the stove and went to his father's bedroom.

Joe Mason was sleeping, and Pete tiptoed in and looked down at his father. It wasn't often that anyone caught the fiercely proud old man off guard. But this was one of the times, and Pete was a little shaken at what he saw. Stripped of its perpetual scowl of defiance and with the keen eyes closed, Joe Mason presented a different image: that of a hurt, tired man against whom stubborn, relentless time was winning its battle.

The cheeks were sunken and there was a pallid cast to the skin that had braved the harsh and frigid reaches of space for so many years. The deep lines Pete had known for so long were even deeper now, showing the extent of his father's suffering since the accident; suffering the old man would have died from rather than admit to.

After studying his father's face for awhile, Pete laid a hand on his shoulder.

"Dad . . ."

Joe Mason's eyes snapped open and he instantly replaced the mask that had dropped away during sleep.

"Oh—Pete. I was resting my eyes a little, waiting for you to come in."

"I overslept, I'm afraid."

"I told Betcha not to wake you up. You're still a growing lad and you need your rest. Here—push this blasted cast so I can sit up."

Pete helped his father into a sitting position. He fully expected a cross-examination as to the previous night's meeting. So he was surprised when his father sat silent for a time, scowling at the wall behind the foot of the bed. Then he suddenly turned his piercing eyes on his son.

"Pete. I want you to go out prospecting."

"Prospecting? Why, Dad, I thought we had some good claims that were just waiting—"

The old man shook his head impatiently. "Not exactly—not exactly. Oh, if we had a full crew and I was on my feet, we could pay the time and cost of working them, but the way things are, we need a richer strike." He'd looked away, but now he glanced quickly back. "We're in no danger of violating the Brotherhood Code. The returns, even if we worked them, would be low enough to justify abandonment. So we'll hold them in reserve for a while, and I want you to go out and hit a big one for us."

"Why, sure, Dad. I can't think of anything I'd rather do."

"Copper prices are good. Hit a nice vein somewhere, and we'll have money to burn."

Pete grinned and hooked his fist across his father's chin in the old man's favorite gesture of affection. "Sure, Dad. Just watch me. In a couple of days I'll come in here and report the biggest strike since Crazy Carter claimed that derelict ship filled with platinum bars."

He was referring to a fabulous Belt incident that had long since become legendary—a miner who'd become a millionaire on a single salvage operation.

"You do that, son," Joe Mason said.

"In the meantime, you just lie there and get well and plan what we'll do with the money."

Pete's smile vanished as he left the bedroom. He passed up breakfast, stowing some dry provender into his monocar, and as he took off into the Belt, his spirits were low.

He moved with the stream and rode comfortably along, thoroughly at home in a world that would have terrorized the native of a solid planet.

An asteroid the size of a football floated along just ahead. Pete approached it, nuzzled it aside with the nose of his monocar, and watched it drift astern.

A larger, more jagged remnant drew alongside and turned itself over for Pete's inspection. It showed clear traces of silver, but unless Pete could discover a larger chunk—the mother asteroid off which it had been broken in collison—it was not worth bothering with.

He was approaching a cluster up ahead, so he nosed left to avoid it and came back on his arbitrary course at the cluster's forward end.

He cruised on. In the temporary lethargy of his low spirits brought on by worry over his father, he ignored the surrounding stream other than to avoid collision, and snapped on his radio. He checked the emergency band as every Beltman automatically did when signaling in, and then switched to the free wave length.

A Federation ship was broadcasting news. There had been an election on Earth for a seat in the World Congress, and a man named Shakari had won. His opponent had immediately cried fraud and demanded a recount.

Such strange goings on, Pete thought. That was how it was on Earth so far as he could see. Everybody fighting tooth and nail for things that didn't seem worth having; at least not to a boy born and raised in the Asteroid Belt. He wondered why the affairs of Earth were of such vital interest to everyone in the System. No, he didn't have to wonder that. It was logical. Earth was the magic center of the System. Everything originated there and everything went back. The ore he was hunting, if he found it, would without doubt find its way to Earth and the money paid for it would come from the big bank vaults down there to buy the supplies the Masons needed to support their existence. Just another circle in the millions of circles, tangible and otherwise, that went to make up the infinite universe.

His mind wandering thus, Pete became aware of a large planetoid above him on the sunside of the Belt. He tilted the monocar's nose and moved in that direction and in a short time he was cruising close, inspecting the planetoid's surface from ten feet.

The planetoid was cone-shaped, its diameter at the top approximately half a mile. That gave a good flat surface for mining operations, and when he set the monocar down and got out, he found enough iron in the rock to hold magnetic boots and grapples. That made everything ideal. Now there was the little matter of enough rich ore to make the operation worthwhile.

Pete was not a pessimist, but he still didn't expect to find anything of value on the planetoid. He based this on experience. There was fabulous wealth still untouched in the Belt, but one man was like an ant searching many acres of desert all alone. Thus, while the wealth was there, it took time to find it, and only sheerest luck would put a prospector on a rich planetoid so quickly.

But it appeared Pete had that luck. Fifteen minutes with a testing kit proved out a copper content in the rock that—against the longest of odds was the strike his father had requested.

Satisfied as to the planetoid's mineral wealth, Pete made the first move toward staking his claim—the plotting of the orbit. This amounted to marketing the location of the asteroid, a simple operation on a major planet, but a complicated one where everything was in bits and pieces and moving in constant stream around the sun. The orbit had to be extremely accurate, a precise notation of the asteroid's movements both within the stream and as a part of it.

Getting his kit from the monocar, he first determined that his rich find was tilted fourteen degrees from the plane of the ecliptic. Using this as the basis of additional calculations, he went on with his work. Time passed because plotting an orbit was not something dashed off in five minutes.

In fact, it was three hours later that Pete put down his final figures, checked them, repacked his kit, and returned to the monocar. Inside, he automatically checked the emergency band on his radio and put down the formula that would enable him to again locate his claim. This was based on the orbital calculations and, if it became practical, the formula could be fed into the radar finder and thus become a part of the monocar's directional equipment, translated as a blip on the screen.

The whole job completed, he rewarded himself by getting out the provender he'd brought with him. This was a dubious reward because the food consisted of some of Betcha Jones's less successful biscuits. Betcha's successful biscuits were nothing to write home about, so the rock-hard consistency of the ones Pete feasted on was easily imagined. But with the

53

tube of jam he'd brought along the biscuits were edible, and he was lifted in spirit by the thought of the good news he would carry to his father. A strike the first time out! You couldn't do any better than that.

He finished his meal, folded the claim data he'd listed on an official blank, and put it in his wallet where it would be safe until filing time.

Then, almost as though it had waited until he was quite ready, a scream came over the emergency band still open on his radio.

"Help! Help! Please—somebody!"

It was a completely "unprofessional" call for assistance by a hysterical female who had reacted in quick terror to some menace—an appalling menace, obviously.

Pete's responses came automatically. "Keep on yelling," he advised, and channeled the screams into his finder. There was a pause with no further screams coming over the wave.

"Are you all right?" Pete asked. "Who are you? State your name and keep repeating it. Give my finder something to work on."

Then the screams came again. "Help! Help! Help!" repeated three times.

This was enough. The finder clicked through its electronic pattern, located the voice, and the beeper began sounding. Ready to move, Pete lifted the car and circled. He checked the beep at two points and found that it led back along the stream and at a thirty-degree tilt from the ecliptic. This pointed him toward what the miners called the Badlands, an area of the

54

Belt where the asteroid pack was thick and jagged—a place generally avoided because it had never yielded much in the way of valuable ore.

The Badlands was a dangerous area to head into recklessly, and Pete would have preferred to stay out of it altogether. But, faced by an emergency, he raced toward the area and began taking risks, any one of which could have smashed his car like the shell of an egg.

Plunging into the dangerous section of the Belt, he noted that the target of the beam was not stationary. That meant the girl was moving; probably fleeing whatever danger menaced her. He wondered if any other cars or ships had gotten the signal.

Then the cry came again. "Help! Please help me!"

"I'm on the way," Pete muttered, and dodged a jagged asteroid just ahead.

The beep, steady and persistent in its electronic per-
fection, led Pete clear through the dangerous rock
stream into comparatively open space beyond. Seemingly annoyed at the imperfection of humans and
their strange antics, the beep angled him several degrees to the left of his previous line of travel and delivered him to a position from which he caught sight
of another monocar.

It was in trouble, its course carelessly erratic. Several times as Pete approached, it turned end-over-end,

lazily, as though no one was at the controls.

The screams had stopped while Pete was still in the rock stream, but he'd been so busy avoiding death that he would have ignored them regardless. But now he called out, "Ahoy! Monocar! I'm overhead! What's your problem?"

The voice that came back was no longer in panic. It was now charged with irritation and hostility. "Well, it took you long enough to get here!"

Pete's mouth dropped open. "Well, for . . . Look! I came as fast as I could. I had to come through the Badlands. Who are you? What happened?"

Who was she! As though Pete didn't know! He hadn't been too sure when he'd picked up the call, but there was no doubt now. He'd again been brought into the orbit of the spitfire from the *Snapdragon*. Jane Barry was in his hair again.

"Well, don't just sit there," she snapped. "Come and help me. I'm losing my air."

"I'll pull alongside and grapple on," Pete said. "Use your belt if you have to."

"What do you think I'm using now—vacuum?"

It was in Pete's mind to ask her if she'd ever spoken a civil word in her life, but he was in the process of easing in to grapple, so he saved the question for later.

Brushing close, he activated the magnetic shoes behind the shell of his car on the right side and the two cars were jerked together.

"You could be a little more careful," Jane complained. "You almost sprained my neck."

I should have broken it, Pete thought. "Sorry," he said. "What did you do—hit a rock?"

57

"It was a ship. An immense thing. It tried to run me down." Echoes of the original fright sounded in Jane's voice.

"You're crazy. There aren't any ships around here."

"It was back there in the Badlands."

"That's even crazier. A ship would have smashed up—even one out of control—before it reached the badlands. An off-course ship might approach the Belt, but . . . well you just blundered into an asteroid and . . ."

"Don't tell me what I did. Do you think I'm blind?"

"As a matter of fact, I was wondering. You hit a rock and call it a ship—"

"Oh, you're impossible! Release your grapples. I'll make it home myself."

"Don't be silly. The way you were staggering, there must be something wrong with your steering vents. How is your heat?"

"It's gone. I'm using my belt."

"The shell of your car is broken then."

"It's cracked."

"Then we'll stay as we are. I'll tow you back to the *Snapdragon*."

There was no reply. Pete set his directionals on Pallas, and the coupled monocars began to move.

There was a time of silence that Jane finally broke. "I tell you it was a ship."

Pete looked out through his plastic shield and into the crippled monocar from which Jane had thrown the angry words into his radio. In no mood to placate or sympathize with her, he snapped, "Oh, be reasonable. So you hit a rock. It's been done before."

"All right. *Don't* believe me!"

"Granted it was, which is ridiculous, you still got very careless. A big ship?"

"Yes. A space liner of some kind. But it was—"

Pete cut in to make his point. "A monocar being put into danger by a space liner is like saying—"

"I know. Maybe I was a little careless. But who would expect a monster like that to come out of nowhere? I just looked up and there is was—filling the whole sky. I jerked my nose down and it banged my tail and almost wrecked me."

"The way you screamed it must have chased you, too."

"I was trapped. The rock stream was thick there. I was blocked in every direction I turned. Then there was that huge hulk grinding down on me. Like—like a live thing."

"Take it easy. You're safe now."

"Then you believe me?"

"I think you believe yourself."

"In other words, I'm feeble-minded."

"You're twisting my words. When people panic—"

"I didn't panic!"

"You should have heard yourself over that emergency band."

"Oh, you're impossible."

Nothing was said for a few moments. Then Pete asked his question. "Tell me something—why are you so hostile?"

"I'm not hostile! I—"

"Oh, cut it out. You haven't said a friendly word since we met."

59

All Pete really expected was more of the same, but Jane didn't flare back at him. He glanced across at her. She sat with her head back on the rest and looked to be tired. Ghost ship or not, she'd had a harrowing experience of some sort and her hostility was at least partially shattered. There was weariness in her face. Pete could see it even behind the headpiece of her oxygen unit.

"You have to be hostile in this world," she said.

"Why?"

"Because that's how it is. My father worked hard all his life and had nothing but bad luck. This is a cold, hostile world out here."

"It isn't so bad."

"No? Just open your shield and step outside and see what happens to you."

"That's silly. It's a dangerous world, sure. But we have safeguards."

"The whole Belt is built to kill you. You've got to be on your toes every minute."

"I think you're just tired. Things will look different in the morning."

"Will they be any better for my mother? It wasn't my father's fault, but what was he able to leave Mother? An old beaten-up ship, a family to raise, no money—"

"It's your younger sisters you're worried about then? And your mother?"

"Wouldn't you worry? Every miner in the Brotherhood hates us."

"That's not true. They just don't like the way your mother does things."

"Well, they can go to blazes!"

"Hold it. Let's not start fighting again."

"I'm sorry."

Pete was amazed. *I'm sorry* coming from Jane Barry was a big concession. For a moment, Pete questioned its sincerity. But it did sound genuine.

"What about your Uncle Homer?"

"What about him?"

"Doesn't he help you? He's part of the family."

"In the first place, he isn't my uncle. He was a very good friend of my father's and so we call him uncle. He can't help much. He has a great deal of bad luck."

Pete was inclined to call it something else. He had a more critical term in mind but, again, he didn't want to ruffle Jane's feathers.

"What were you doing out in the Belt?"

"I was prospecting."

"That's no job for a girl."

"I've got as much right as anybody else to."

"No, take it easy. Of course you have. But you didn't expect to find anything in the Badlands, did you?"

"Who knows where rich ore lies in the Belt? It could be there just as easily as any place else."

"Except that it's generally agreed that it isn't. All those rocks came from the same source. It's a smashed-up planet that drifted into the stream."

Jane didn't choose to argue the point. She was silent for awhile. Her eyes were closed, and Pete thought she was taking a nap. Then she proved herself to be awake by saying, "I've got to get this car fixed and then go back and find that crazy ship."

She'd certainly seen something, Pete realized. But

what had it really been? A ship blundering around in the Badlands would get into trouble immediately and radio for help. A call from a space liner would have brought every miner in the sector, hoping for salvage money.

Seeking to change the subject and take Jane's mind off her near-fatal accident, Pete said, "I struck it rich today. I found an asteroid dripping with copper."

"Congratulations. I hope my call didn't pull you away from your work."

"I was finished when it came in. I'd already chartered the orbit and made out the claim form. It's here in my pocket."

"Now all you have to do is file."

Pete suddenly wished he hadn't mentioned the claim. He didn't like the wistful note in Jane's voice. But then he quickly told himself he was being unfair. Jane wasn't a thief. Neither was her mother. Then he suddenly wondered if Rachel and her brood were not unjustly suffering from Homer's reputation.

"You say that Uncle Homer, as you call him, was a good friend of your father's."

"Yes. When Father was alive, he depended on Uncle Homer a great deal. They worked together—mined together."

"I wonder if it wasn't the other way around."

"What do you mean?"

"Maybe Uncle Homer depended a lot on your father."

"You're not making sense. Father was wonderful. But he was . . . well, very impractical."

"Yes, but from what I've heard he was also one of

the best mining engineers in the Belt. He had both the knowledge and the instinct."

"That was true," Jane said proudly.

"And yet he never came away with much wealth."

Jane frowned and turned her eyes to look through the two glass panels that separated them. "What are you driving at?"

"I've also heard that your father was so honest he couldn't cheat anybody if he'd wanted to, and sometimes people like that think everybody is as honest, too."

Jane's eyes sparked dangerously. "If you're saying what I think you're saying . . ."

"I'm only pointing out a possibility based on things I've heard. The stories I've heard about things going wrong for your father every time he was on the verge of a real bonanza. Of course, it's none of my business, but—"

"That's exactly right, *Mister* Mason. It's none of your business!"

Pete raised a quick hand. "All right—all right. I apologize. I was out of line."

"You certainly were! Release your grapples. I'll get home by myself!"

"Oh, not that again. Why don't you grow up and start controlling those childish tantrums? If I let go you'd start wallowing all over the Belt."

The truth of this had a dampening effect on Jane. She hesitated and Pete followed up his advantage.

"Truce?"

"All right—truce."

Pete felt that he had the picture. Jane had adored

63

her father. In her eyes he could have done no wrong of any description and now that he was gone she accepted as absolute truth all the explanations for failure he had ever given his family. Thus, her father's belief that Uncle Homer was a loyal friend had become Jane's belief also.

In a strange, twisted way, Uncle Homer had become Jane's father image.

"I'll not mention Uncle Homer again," Pete said, "if you'll tell me one thing."

"Tell you what?"

"Do you get any help at all from him?"

He thought she was going to flare again, but she didn't. Still, there was defiance in her voice as she said, "He tries. Uncle Homer tries very hard and one of these days he'll hit his bonanza and then everything will be fine."

"That's great. So why are you worrying about your family? All you have to do is hang on."

"Oh, will you shut up?"

Pete turned his head away to hide a small grin. He felt he'd won something in his personality war with Jane Barry. He couldn't figure out exactly what, though. And while he was mulling it over, a shape more symmetrical than an asteroid loomed in the light from the distant sun, and he said, "Look, there's the *Snapdragon*."

Jane looked but had no comment, and Pete said, "Seeing you coming home this way—being towed— will probably scare your mother."

"No. She'd be more scared if I came in end-over-end without a tow."

"That's logical."

Pete eased the two cars toward the starboard air-lock of the *Snapdragon*. She was a tired old ship, a Class Five space freighter that limped along at speeds that were now minor, but which had been major fifty years earlier. She was limited to an inner-stellar orbit because the passengers in a ship of her class would have become very old while traveling a single light-year.

While Jane was clearing the crippled monocar, Pete saw two small faces pressed against the quartz of the portholes on either side of the airlock. They would belong to Ellen and Colleen, Jane's younger sisters, and they weren't in the least panicked by the sight of Jane coming home crippled. The younger one was giggling, and the older one brazenly winked at Pete and then stuck her tongue out.

"You're all right now," Pete said. "I'll anchor your car to the hull and go on my way."

"You can't do that. You have to come in for at least a few minutes."

"I don't have much time. I want to get to the Federation office at Parma and file my claim."

"But Mother will think you're slighting us."

"You know that isn't true."

"Yes, but she doesn't."

"All right. But just for a few minutes."

The two younger Barrys were eagerly awaiting their guest just beyond the inner door of the airlock. They were both dark, like Jane, and had the flashing Barry eyes. But while Ellen, the twelve-year-old, was slim and graceful, the younger Colleen was a butterball. And they were both as frank and forthright as their elder sister.

"I know you," Colleen announced. "You're one of the miners. You hate us."

"I do not," Pete protested.

"You do too," Ellen chimed in. "You're always try-ing to keep us from making a living!"

"Why, I wouldn't do that for all the gold in the Belt."

"You're just saying that to be polite."

"Ellen!" Jane said, "you stop that. Where's Mother?"

"She's in the bedroom reading her astrology book."

"Did you tell her I was towed in?"

"No. She's casting her horoscope for all next week. We never interrupt her when she's doing that."

"Mother never moves until she finds out which way the stars point," Jane said by way of explanation. "Pardon me while I make a cup of tea."

She left the room, and it occurred to Pete that he had referred to it that way in his mind. A *room*. But spaceships didn't have rooms, they had cabins. That was what made the *Snapdragon* different. There was a rug on the floor of this particular room and a big easy chair into which he dropped to await developments.

There were pictures on the walls and curtains in the windows—except that in a ship the walls were bulk-heads and the windows were ports, thus making things very confusing.

One thing was certain. Rachel Barry, whatever else she'd done, had made a home for her little brood.

Ellen regarded Pete narrowly from a safe distance while Colleen, less particular about whom she associ-ated with, climbed into his lap.

"I like you—I think," she said.

"I like you for sure," Pete answered.

"Did you come here to spy on us?"

"No. I brought your sister home."

"When Uncle Homer's here, he says never answer the door, because it would be somebody spying."

That was interesting, but Pete reserved comment. "Do you like living in a spaceship?"

"She's never lived anywhere else," Ellen said.

"What about you?"

"I lived on Parma for awhile—in a house."

"She doesn't remember it, though. She was too small. What's that?"

Colleen had reached into Pete's pocket and taken out his slide rule. He'd put it there while computing the orbit of the claim he'd found. "It's something to work out problems on. Haven't you ever seen one before?"

"That's nothing," Ellen sniffed. "Jane uses one when she plots a course for the *Snapdragon*."

"I'll bet she doesn't use it as good as you do," Colleen said, then, obviously a child of impulse and quick affection, she threw her arms around Pete and planted a wet kiss on his cheek.

Pete laughed. "Hey, hold it. You're a pretty fast worker."

"I love you," Colleen said and clung with all her might.

"Don't pay any attention to her," Ellen said. "She loves everybody."

But it was impossible not to pay attention to Colleen. She refused to let go, and Pete, trying to dislodge her as gently as possible, came to his feet.

Instantly, Ellen leaped forward and flung herself upon him. He went to his knees and and both the young Barrys whooped with delight. Finding himself

68

smothered, Pete struggled blindly, the impetuous pair too much for him on such short notice. Then his prayer for help was answered.

"Ellen—Colleen! Get up off that floor. I'm ashamed of you."

"Aw, Mom. We were just showing Pete how to wrestle."

They untangled themselves and drew away and Pete got back on his feet. "Thanks, Mrs. Barry," he grinned. "They were too much for me."

"Girls," she scolded. "You're too young to call older people by their first names. This is *Mister* Mason."

"Jane called him Pete," Ellen complained.

"She's older than you are," Rachael Barry said, as Pete brushed carpet lint off his jacket. "Please sit down, Pete," She sighed. "It's so very difficult, raising three healthy, active children without a father."

"I can sympathize with you."

"It was so nice of you to drop in. Jane should be home before long. She went out to do a little prospecting."

"She's here now. I came with her."

"Oh, that's nice. By the way, Pete, when were you born?"

"In August. The ninth."

"That makes you a Leo. That's a very good sign."

"Jane's in the kitchen making tea, Mom," Ellen said.

"I'll bet she's in the bathroom fixing up her hair. When she comes out she'll be wearing a dress and her hair will be all combed."

"Jane had a little accident," Pete said, pushing his

69

words in between those of the Barry girls. "I towed her home."

"Oh, that was nice of you. So neighborly. I wish the miners were more neighborly."

"It's just that everyone is so busy making a living. Then too, not many of them are married. Mining is a pretty rough life for wives."

"That's what I keep telling everyone," Rachel Barry said.

Pete wished Jane would come back. He didn't feel at ease with Rachel, not being used to the company of females.

At the moment he was struck by Rachel's apparent lack of interest in Jane's accident. This seemed inconsistent with her reputation as a devoted mother to the Barry brood. Then, possessing a certain insight into people, he realized that Rachel had a sublime faith in destiny. You worked and did your best, and destiny would see to it that nothing really bad ever happened.

Then he learned another thing about his hostess. When she wanted something, she asked for it. "Pete," Rachel said, "we want to move the *Snapdragon* closer to the main stream of the Belt. That will make it easier for Jane to prospect."

Pete almost said that a seventeen-year-old girl had no business prospecting for ore in the first place, but he remembered that it was none of his business.

"It's so far from Pallas to the good fields. Will you help us?"

"Move the ship, you mean?"

"Yes. Jane and I can do it, of course, but we really need a man to help."

70

"What about Homer? I'd think that—"

"Oh, Homer is a dear, but he has so many problems of his own. A body can't depend on him."

"Why, I'd be glad to help."

That wasn't true. Pete wasn't glad at all. He had his own work and he felt that it was Homer's job. But he could hardly refuse in the face of Rachel Barry's direct request.

"Do you think your father would mind if we moored some place on Juno? It's a very big planetoid and we'd be no trouble at all."

"I'm sure he wouldn't mind," Pete replied.

What was he saying? Joe Mason would go straight through the ceiling of his slab-aluminum bedroom!

"Why, that's so sweet of you," Rachel said. "Your offer is *most* kind. And you'll hardly know we're there."

Not know the Barrys were around? That was really rubbing it in. Pete gulped. He'd been about to reverse himself, or at least tell Rachel Barry he'd have to ask his father first. But after her outpouring of gratitude, he couldn't find the words.

"It's nothing," he murmured.

Then he was hit from two sides by the Barry offspring as they demonstrated their gratitude in what amounted to physical attack. Advancing from two sides, they threw themselves on him.

"We love you! We love you!" they shrieked.

And as they began taking Pete apart, Rachel Barry beamed happy approval. "You've made a tremendous impression on them. They're usually quite shy with strangers."

71

Pete couldn't conceive Ellen and Colleen as being shy with anyone, but he was too busy defending himself from the violent affection of the two extroverts to give much thought to the idea of their being shy.

Then he got his next surprise. This came as Colleen caught sight of someone or something in the doorway and hurled herself off Pete's lap.

"Here's Omaha," she cried. "He wants to thank you too."

She rushed toward the door. Pete's eyes followed and he saw a small, furry beast glaring balefully at him from the doorway. It was on four squat legs and had a tail it kept twitching nervously. It looked as though it would enjoy having him for dinner.

The eyes were its most arresting feature. A clear ice-blue, they contrasted with its long, black, silky coat and made Pete think of two sharp knives pointed at his heart.

"What's—that," he gulped.

Rachel Barry laughed gently. "You've certainly heard of Omaha. He's our pet cat. We all love him and he loves us."

"Omaha's famous," Colleen babbled. "Daddy got him on Mars the last time he went there."

"Somebody brought him from Earth," Ellen said. "That's where they have cats. He's the only one in the Belt."

"Oh, sure. I've heard of Omaha. He just—well, surprised me."

Ellen picked the beast up and ran back to Pete's chair. "Here. He wants to sit in your lap."

This wasn't true. Omaha had no desire whatever to

72

sit in Pete's lap. The beast's hair stood on end. Its red mouth opened, revealing many sharp white teeth.

It did not use these, however. It had other, more convenient weapons: sharp claws on its feet. A thick, hissing sound rasped from its throat as it lashed out with the claws. They bit deep into Pete's sleeve as Omaha made a seemingly impossible backward leap and landed on the floor in front of the chair.

"Why, Omaha," Rachel Barry said sternly. "That's no way to treat a guest."

"You hurt him," Ellen accused. "You pinched him or something!"

"I did not!" Pete retorted.

"I think he's frightened," Colleen said wisely.

This didn't appear likely from where Pete sat. The beast crouched in front of his chair and appeared ready to take on all comers regardless of size and weight.

"It takes a little time with animals," Rachel Barry said gently.

At that moment, Jane came to Pete's rescue carrying a tray full of tea things. She wore a dress and her black hair had been brushed until it glowed like silk.

"Beat it, Omaha," she said, and the cat lifted its tail and retired from the field in contemptuous triumph.

"Tea! How lovely!" Rachel said. "You see, Pete, we do preserve the amenities on the *Snapdragon* even under difficulties."

"Oh, Mother. Stop it!" Jane said. "I made a cup of tea. What's so tremendous about that?"

"Pete tells me you had an accident, dear."

73

"I hit a ship in the Badlands."

The sensational aspects of this statement escaped Rachel completely. Her mind was elsewhere. "Wasn't it nice to have a strong man come to your rescue?"

Jane's eyes narrowed. Pete, watching her, admired the willpower she displayed by not only holding her temper but smiling and replying sweetly, "Yes, Mother—very nice." Then Jane turned her eyes on Pete, the smile remaining. "You're probably beginning to understand why we don't have much company on the *Snapdragon*."

Completely bemused by the Barrys, Pete sipped his tea and wondered what would happen next. His cup empty, he said, "I've got to hurry along. It's been great and I wish I could stay longer, but it's getting late."

"Do come again," Rachel said. Her motherly smile radiated out to include Pete in the family group. "Jane," she said, "Pete has invited us to moor the *Snapdragon* on Juno."

Jane's mouth dropped open as she stared at her mother.

"He—*what?*"

"He invited us to moor on Juno. He even volunteered to help us move the ship."

Jane turned her gaze on Pete, but he dropped his eyes. "I *do* have to go," he murmured.

"I'll open the lock for you," Jane said grimly.

"Goodbye, Pete," Rachel smiled placidly. "It's been so nice having you."

The younger pair had already left in search of Omaha, and Rachel departed also. Jane went to the

74

lock, checked the air gauge, and opened it. She turned and faced Pete.

"What really happened?"

Pete did a pretty good job of looking innocent. "Why, it was like your Mother said—"

"It was not! Quit trying to be a gentleman. It doesn't look good on you. She asked to go to Juno and she asked you to help us. Isn't that right?"

"Well—"

"Tell the truth."

Pete's anger flared. He was the victim of this conspiracy. He'd done the decent thing for Rachel Barry and now her daughter was blaming him for it.

"All right. We'll forget the whole thing," Pete said. "It will be a great relief to me not to have to ask Dad about the *Snapdragon* mooring on Juno. Tell your mother I changed my mind on both counts."

Jane's snapping black eyes glittered dangerously. "We've got a perfect legal right to moor on Juno. You didn't stake claims on the whole surface."

In truth, the Masons had staked only one small claim on their home asteroid. Their rights were of a somewhat different nature.

"We have possessor's rights to that asteroid, and you know it."

"There's nothing in the law about possessors. They don't legally exist."

"Everybody in the Belt recognizes them. The miner who settles a planetoid and puts up a dwelling place has total rights."

"All right. Then why isn't it the same on Parma?

Miners live there and don't claim they own the whole asteroid."

"Parma is a community planetoid—the biggest in the section, as you well know."

"And Juno is the third biggest. There's no reason why you Masons should have the whole thing."

"If that's the way you feel about it, why did your mother ask permission? Why didn't she just moor on it?"

Quite suddenly—without a moment's warning— Jane burst into tears. This, at best, was a foolish thing to do in the cruel atmosphere—or, rather, lack of atmosphere in the Belt. The heating equipment used outside sheltered areas was constructed to hold against the merciless cold, but tears froze instantly.

Appalled, Pete exclaimed, "Stop it! Do you want to blind yourself?"

Acting on instinct, he seized Jane by the arm, opened the plastic bubble of his monocar and pulled her inside. He slammed the bubble shut and turned the heat gauge to top capacity.

"Keep your eyes closed," he said.

Frightened, Jane made no resistance as Pete turned her face upward to check for possible tissue damage.

"How do your eyes feel?"

"They feel all right."

"I guess you got them closed in time. Can you open them?"

"No."

They were frozen shut, of course, but there had probably been no damage to the eyeballs.

76

"Just relax. And breathe through your mouth so you won't pull the ice in your nostrils in deeper when it thaws. Of all the crazy tricks!"

The tears that had run down Jane's cheeks were solid ice. Using his fingernail, Pete carefully lifted the droplets away. They left white spots where they had instantly congealed.

"You could have gone blind in less than a minute!"

"Do you think I don't know that?"

"Then why did you start bawling?"

"Men are fools!" Jane replied, this being her answer to Pete's lack of understanding.

"I'd say it's the other way around. I never saw a man do a stupid thing like that. Why doesn't your mother take you to Mars where you belong?"

"We've got just as much right . . . !"

"Okay! Okay! Forget I asked."

"Let me out of here!"

Crowded into a car meant for only one, they were packed tight against each other. Jane began to struggle. The car rocked.

"Cut it out!" Pete snapped. "I don't like this any better than you do. But until your nostrils get clear of ice and your eyes dry out, you're going to stay here."

Fighting more tears, Jane turned her face away. Their headpieces were down, the monocar unit having taken over, and Jane sniffled faintly. She said nothing, and Pete couldn't put any words together either. So they sat there, both of them angry, miserable, and completely frustrated.

"Do you feel better?" Pete finally asked.

"I feel all right."

"We'll wait another couple of minutes. Then you can go back into your ship."

Another period of silence followed before Jane said, "I'm sorry."

It was the second time she'd admitted to being wrong, and Pete should have found satisfaction therein. But he did not find anything but annoyance. Why, he wondered, did he—practically a stranger— have to get involved with this weird family? He wasn't hostile to them. He wished them all the good luck imaginable, but he had problems of his own without taking on theirs. Since he was in this spot, though, he had to be decent about it.

"I think I can talk Dad into letting you moor on Juno."

"Thank you," Jane said contritely. "It doesn't make any difference to me one way or another—you understand that, don't you?"

"Of course."

"But if Mother wants to moor there—" Jane cut off in mid-sentence, her face turning thoughtful.

"What's the matter?" Pete asked.

"I wonder why?"

"Why what?"

"Why Mother wants to moor on Juno. There are plenty of other asteroids if she's tired of this one."

"There's no ore on Juno."

"You mean you think my Mother plans to get all you—?"

"No," Pete cut in quickly. "I didn't mean that at all."

He'd learned how defensive she was—how quickly

her anger flared and he preferred her in a reasonable mood.

"The things the Brotherhood says—"

"I'm not the Brotherhood. I wish you'd understand that. I'm Pete Mason and I don't go by what other people say."

"Are you two having a nice conversation?"

The question came from the monocar speaker in warm, motherly tones that identified them as originating inside the *Snapdragon*. Rachel Barry was encouraging "neighborliness" and, when he turned to look toward the *Snapdragon*, Pete saw the two younger Barrys with their faces again glued to the ports. They were reacting with high glee to the sight of Pete and Jane wedged into the monocar. How, Pete asked himself, had he ever managed to get Uncle Homer into it the previous night?"

"You'd better explain to your mother why you're in here," Pete said as he raised his headpiece preparatory to opening the bubble.

"She'd only worry," Jane said.

It was difficult for Pete to concede the truth of that statement. It didn't appear to him that Rachel Barry worried as much as she was assumed to. He thought he detected a sublime faith in destiny there. While not bashful in her requests, Rachel Barry appeared to believe that everything would turn out all right if given enough time and a few appropriate nudges.

Jane said, "Thanks for helping me," and began to climb out of the car. She wasn't using her magnets and, as she reached out to grasp the anchor bar beside the *Snapdragon*'s air lock, a second monocar dropped down to the asteroid's surface. As Pete closed his bubble, he glanced in that direction and saw Uncle Homer at the controls. Not wishing to be delayed any longer, Pete raised a hand in salute and lifted his own car away. Evidently Uncle Homer had successfully escaped the wrath of his accuser at the Brotherhood meeting. He wondered how long Homer could continue making such escapes.

As he lifted away from the cold, bleak surface of Pallas, Pete felt a touch of guilt. This came from the realization that he had not contacted the *Windjammer* all day.

Earlier, he'd thought of relaying the good news, but then he'd decided it would be more fun to walk in, after filing the claim, and casually announce the results of his single day's work. Betcha's grudging approval would be most pleasant, he'd told himself.

But the necessity of rescuing Jane had disrupted

everything, and now there was just time to reach the Federation office on Parma and file his claim.

Hoping his father hadn't worried too much, Pete snapped the switch and gave the *Windjammer*'s call letters. The gruff voice of Betcha Jones came back.

"What are you doing out there, boy? It's a good idea to report in once in a while."

"Sorry, Betcha. I got very busy. How's Dad?"

"He's too healthy to be down and not healthy enough to be up." Betcha turned his voice away and Pete heard him say, "He's finally come in, Joe. Says he was busy."

"Are you all right, Pete?" It was Joe Mason's voice, sharp with concern.

"I'm fine, Dad. I made a real strike! Copper! We can put a full crew to work."

"Cocky kids—" This was Betcha's sour comment. "Goes out and makes a strike in a few hours. Of course it'll turn out to be a dud, but—"

"It will not! It's a thick vein of high-grade ore. We can work the whole asteroid!"

"What's the topography, son?" Joe Mason asked.

"Ideal, Dad. Cone-shaped and smooth. Plenty of anchorage surface. Maximum return with minimum effort. I'm on the way to Parma now."

"Okay, son. Call us when you get there."

It was significant that neither of the men asked the asteroid's location. The radio channels were open to everyone in the Belt, and in even describing the asteroid's shape Pete could have said too much. But he was less than an hour from filing, so he'd decided it was safe to reassure his father.

"All right, Dad. And Betcha—make a big pot of stew. I'll be plenty hungry when I get back."

Pete cut off the channel and spent the intervening time thinking about the Barrys. The only thing really wrong with them was Rachel Barry's mistakes in judgment—keeping a family of girls out here in an environment that was a challenge to strong and experienced men. She could have sold the *Snapdragon* and gotten enough to establish her growing family in one of the Martian communities. There was work for women there. Rachel Barry could have set up an apparel shop for one thing. The wives and daughters of the Martian colonists were hungry for fashionable clothes, for new things, and they had plenty of money. With a little wisely directed initiative, Rachel could locate on Mars and send them all to schools on Earth. It was a shame that Jane had to waste her early years in a place like the Belt.

He became so preoccupied with the injustice that he almost overshot Parma, dropping down just in time to keep from missing the settlement where the Federation office was located. He moored his car and hurried into the building with just about enough time left to file his claim.

The greeting he received from the young man behind the desk was not enthusiastic. A blond youth with a faraway look in his eyes, he was easily identified for what he was—a native Earthling—a career man in the vast Federation who'd drawn the dreariest of assignments as an apprenticeship—a temporary exile on this airless, soilless rock far from the fabled green hills of Earth. And even though the attractions of Earth were strictly objective to Pete and thus not greatly attractive, the young man still had Pete's sympathy. Pete got a concept of how he felt by reversing the thing. Suppose he, Pete Mason, were exiled on the big central planet far from the free, robust life in the Belt. He would be miserable!

"I've got a claim to file," Pete said as he pulled off his gloves.

The young man glanced at his wrist chronometer. "It's pretty late."

"There's still time to file, though."

"Yes. And I've got no place to go anyhow."

"I've got the orbit of the claim plotted and entered on a claim form." Pete plunged a hand into his pocket. A blank look wiped the smile from his face. The clerk looked at him questioningly.

"What's wrong?"

"It's gone."

"Maybe you put it in a different pocket."

He watched as Pete started going through his other pockets. Finally, as a gesture of despair, he took out his wallet and examined the contents, although he knew he hadn't put the claim form into it.

The clerk was mildly sympathetic. "You couldn't possibly have those figures in your head?"

"I'm not a genius," Pete said ruefully.

"Can you locate the claim again?"

"Oh, sure. I remember the section markings and the stream location bearings."

"It takes a lot more than that to file a claim. I guess you'll have to do it all over again."

"I guess you're right."

84

"We'll be open all day tomorrow."

"I stopped to tow a disabled car home," Pete spoke just on the edge of anger. "Otherwise everything would have been all right."

"Maybe you can claim salvage. That way the day won't be a total loss."

"Fat chance. The people I towed haven't got anything to pay it with."

The clerk shrugged. "Then you've stored up treasure in heaven. You'll have to settle for that."

"At least until tomorrow. I'll see you then."

"I'll be here," the young man said wearily.

"You must have just thought you put it in your pocket," Betcha Jones said. "It would be there otherwise. You went straight to the claim office—"

"Well—not exactly."

"Not exactly? Where did you go?"

"I towed a disabled monocar."

Betcha scowled and began tapping his boot on the floor. "Well, that's interesting. You found a car floating along in the stream—"

"No. There was someone in it."

"Who was in it, son?" Joe Mason asked.

"Jane Barry."

"Well, great gadgets!" Betcha marveled. "You make a strike and it just happens that one of the Barrys, the finest pirates in the business, is drifting by at the moment in a crippled car."

"No. I answered a call. She was way across the stream—in the Badlands. A big space liner hit her there."

85

"A space liner—in the Badlands. It gets thicker and thicker. I'll betcha it had pink spots on it, and the jets were done up in blue ribbons."

"That was her story, and I didn't believe it either, but her car was disabled."

Joe Mason waved an impatient hand. "What else could he do?" Then to Pete, "Did you lose the claim form on the way?"

"Of course he didn't," Betcha snorted. "She made eyes at him and swiped it."

"I went in with her for a cup of tea."

Betcha gaped in amazement. "Well, glory be to Leo, if that isn't—"

"Go get the boy something to eat," Joe Mason snapped. "He's had a hard day and he's hungry."

Betcha got up and grumbled his way to the bedroom door. Soon he was slamming pots around in the kitchen.

"Do you think they picked your pocket, son?"

"No, Dad. I honestly don't think the Barrys are dishonest. I mean—well, she is a lone woman trying to raise a family—"

"What about Homer?"

"I don't know about Homer."

"Was he there when you were?"

"He came as I was leaving."

"I heard there was some trouble at the meeting last night."

"Yes, I didn't get a chance to tell you. Milt Blaney accused Homer. He said Homer was one of three men who raided his claim and shot him." Pete almost added his suspicions of Homer Barry. But his father was quick to flare, so Pete decided to wait for more concrete evidence. Unnecessary excitement at the moment would serve no purpose.

"You helped Homer escape."

"Yes—yes, I did. It seemed the right thing to do."

"It was, Pete." Joe Mason stopped to scowl and Pete was struck by what he could only term as his father's new mildness. Not mild exactly, but that was the best word Pete could think of. The inherent storminess had gone out of Joe Mason. This was a mixed blessing for Pete. His father was more gentle and understanding now, but this might also indicate that his injuries from the accident were more than physical; that his morale had become a matter of concern.

"It was the right thing to do," Joe Mason repeated. "Charges of that kind should be made to the authorities, not in front of a bunch of hot-headed miners."

"That's the way I felt about it."

"Now—what about the claim form? Where do you think you lost it?"

"I don't know. I was wrestling with the Barry children when I visited their ship. Maybe . . ."

Joe Mason's eyebrows went up. "I didn't know you knew them that well."

"I don't—I didn't, that is. They're—well, they kind of move in and climb all over you. I'll call and ask them if—"

"I wouldn't do that. They found it or they didn't. Calling won't change that. It would only make them realize how important it is."

"You still think they're thieves."

"I didn't say that. But I think it would be smarter to

keep your business to yourself. Go back and rework the orbit tomorrow and take it straight to the claim office."

"I'd better not wait. I'd better do it right now."

"You've had a long day. Get some rest first. We can't have you running yourself down and getting sick."

Pete obeyed, mainly to humor his father. Again, a different Joe Mason had been reflected, and as he ate his dinner and got into bed, Pete wondered about advancing years and their affect on people. He never talked about such things and even his father was not aware of this serious streak in his nature. But it was not beyond Pete's scope to think about such things. The older people got, it seemed to him, the less sure of themselves they became.

It followed then, he thought, that fathers got comfort and satisfaction from seeing themselves in their sons; that a son listening to his father and gaining from the experience and wisdom of years was not just a smart thing to do. It was a duty.

As he drifted off to sleep, his thoughts went elsewhere; back to his day with the crazy Barrys. That bunch'll get me in trouble, he told himself. Stay clear of them.

But even at that point, a small voice deep inside told him it might not work out that way.

Pete slept five hours and when he opened his eyes, he was wide awake. The house was still except for Betcha's healthy snores. The racket was helpful in a way. It covered the small sounds Pete made as he got dressed, left the house, and headed for his new-found claim. He fed the data he remembered into his finder and set his course. And even though he was sure of his figures, he was still relieved when, two hours later, the cone-shaped asteroid came into view on the sunside just as it had appeared previously.

Resolving to let nothing divert him from his job this time, he set down on the broad, flat surface and again went to work on the orbit. This being the second time around, the operation went faster. But it was still three hours before he finished filling in the second form and lifted his monocar into the Parma arc.

He had some bad luck in transit. The location of Parma was against the Belt stream in relation to his claim, and he was challenged by a jagged cluster that had drifted into the channel. It was too thick to thread without data on its formation, so Pete went around it, thus losing another two hours. So it was high noon—Belt time—when he sat down on Parma and entered the Federation claim office.

The blond youth was behind the desk. A night's sleep hadn't cheered him up any; his manner as wearily resigned as before.

Pete laid his claim form on the desk. "Here it is. A new one. Now we can get this filing business over with."

"Of course," the blond young man agreed. He took four additional forms from the neat piles behind him and handed them to Pete. "Just fill these out while I register the orbit."

Pete crossed the room to a desk and sat down to his work. He'd never filed a claim before, but the process was a familiar one. He'd watched his father do it many times.

He'd worked for perhaps fifteen minutes when the clerk called to him from the desk. "Mr. Mason, would you please step over here a moment?"

Pete went back to the desk, his eyes questioning.

"There seems to be some mistake," the clerk said. "This is a duplicate filing."

"Why, that's crazy! What do you mean—duplicate?"

"A claim on this location was legally filed at nine o'clock this morning.

"That's impossible!"

"Nevertheless, it's true. The orbits are identical, and we both know that two claims cannot occupy the same space at the same time."

If this was an attempt at humor, it was lost on Pete. "Who—what—when—?" he sputtered. "Who filed the other claim? When did—?"

"There were three men waiting for me when I opened the office this morning. They had their claim forms all filled out and ready."

"Who signed the affidavit?"

The clerk turned away for a moment. "I have it right here. The man's name was—Homer Deeds."

Uncle Homer! Maybe his last name was Deeds, but that didn't hide his identity. He was one of the Barry clan, and they were at it again! Here was the proof! They had deliberately and cold-bloodedly jumped the Mason claim!

"It's all legal and—and finished—right?"

"I'm afraid so. This gentleman beat you to it." Noting the dazed expression on Pete's face, the clerk said, "Of course, you can file a protest and the Federation referee will hear both sides and rule on it but . . ."

That *but* was most eloquent. The clerk was really saying, Why bother? Unless a criminal act or a criminal conspiracy could be glaringly proven, the duly filed prior claim was invariably favored. And even then the investigation took so long that a man could grow old waiting for a decision.

Pete stared at the offending claim form. Then he said, "I'll have to think this over," and walked slowly out of the claim office.

The bald theft shocked him to a point where he forgot a gesture that should have been automatic—he did not snap on his heat unit. Five steps beyond the door the hundred-degree-minus temperature of the Belt hit him like a steel wall. He came out of his daze and snapped on the unit, but after he got back into his monocar it still took five minutes to get the deep chill out of his bones.

His normal blood flow having returned, he tuned his radio into the public channel and sent out the Mason call letters.

Betcha's rasping voice came back to him. "Pete? Where the devil are you? Why didn't you wake me up? Your Dad's worried because you went out without breakfast."

"Is Dad awake?"

"Awake? He's trying to crawl out of that cast."

"Let me talk to him."

There was a pause and Joe Mason's voice cut in. "What is it, son?"

"Our claim was jumped."

Under the old circumstances that would have been

enough to bring Joe Mason roaring onto Parma with all jets blazing. Even now, he didn't take the news casually. "Jumped? What sneaking son of a renegade asteroid had the nerve to jump a Mason claim?"

"Take it easy, Dad. There's no point in getting excited. Just quiet down and I'll tell you about it."

Pete sensed the effort his father exerted in complying with the suggestion. "All right, son. So we got jumped. Tell me about it."

"I just came from the office. The claim was filed this morning. Three men were waiting when the clerk opened up."

"Who were they?"

"Uncle Homer signed the affidavit. That's Homer Barry, except that his name is—"

"Deeds!"

"You knew that?"

"Certainly. I've known it for years. But what difference does it make? You're right. He's a Barry and they're all as crooked as a blind man's mine shaft!"

"I'm heading for the *Snapdragon* now. I'm going to have this out once and for all."

"Wait a minute, son."

"What do you mean? What's there to wait for?"

Joe Mason's tone and temper had changed. "What did you just tell me? There's no point in getting excited. All right. I want you to take your own advice. Quiet down."

"Sure I said that. But you're down in bed. What I meant was—"

"You just listen to what I mean—"

"But Dad! We got jumped! We're in the right!"

92

"Sure. But you can be just as dead as if you were in the wrong. A bullet doesn't care who it hits."

"What are you talking about?"

"Use your head, Pete! Aren't these sure to be the same men you heard about at the meeting? They've already shot one miner. And it might have been their ship I saw after I got that load of shale."

"I've had that in mind for quite a while. Now I'm convinced."

"All right. But they're dangerous and I don't want you getting hurt. Go to the Brotherhood hall. There are always a few miners hanging around there. Tell them the story and they'll arm themselves and go with you and you can blast your way into the *Snapdragon* and make your own justice."

Pete was stunned for a second time that day. "Dad! Have you gone crazy? Go out there and turn guns on those kids?"

"No. I haven't gone crazy. But I thought for a minute that you had."

Jarred back to sober thinking, Pete's sense of humor came to his rescue as his imagination conjured up a picture of little Colleen poking a gun through the airlock of the *Snapdragon* and letting him have it.

"What are you chuckling at?" Joe Mason asked.

"Nothing Dad. But you're right. We've got to be sensible about this thing. What do you want me to do?"

There was a long pause. Pete wondered if his father had heard him. Then, just as he was about to repeat the question, Joe Mason replied. He spoke very quietly. "I'm leaving that up to you, son."

93

"But Dad—"

"When I said you had to take over for the Masons, I didn't mean I wanted you to just be my messenger boy, doing what I tell you to do. You make the decisions now. I'll back you in anything you do—and I mean anything. If you decide violence is the answer, Betcha and the men and I will back the play. It's up to you."

"You don't think it's a good idea, though."

"No."

"Then what do you . . . ?"

"I'll give you advice—if you ask for it."

"No," Pete replied suddenly and definitely. "Let me think it over first."

"That's the idea. Sit back and sort things out in your mind and then make your decision."

"I'll call you back, Dad. In the meantime, see to it that Betcha doesn't go out on a rampage and get himself killed."

"Right, son. I'll keep him under control."

Pete cut out of the channel, warmed by the pride in his father's voice. Then he sat back in the monocar seat and applied himself totally to the problem.

The first thought that came to him was his confusion as to Homer Deed's exact relationship with the Barrys. He was considered to be a member of the Barry clan and yet—even with what had happened— Pete couldn't see the other Barrys as openly criminal claim jumpers. He'd gotten a certain insight into Jane Barry's character and personality during the short time they'd been together, and he felt he had at least a clue to the situation. But how should he proceed?

He could go straight to the authorities and lodge a formal complaint. That would put the whole matter out of his hands and he could sit back—perhaps for months—and see what developed. Or he could face Homer directly and make a personal issue of the theft.

He knew that was what his father would have done in the old days. But it was also what he now advised against. Or did he? Perhaps not. Maybe he only wanted Pete to be sure of himself.

Then another thought—a somewhat happier one—struck Pete. He rolled it around in his mind. He liked it. He grinned. Then, turning from thought to action, he left the monocar and went back into the Federation building.

But to a different office this time. The lettering on the door he opened read:

Dept. of Salvage Plans & Claims

This office was laid out pretty much like the other. The same desk, the same furniture, the same picture of the System Capitol dome on the wall. The only difference was the color of the clerk's hair. It was black, but he wore the same expression of martyred exile as did his blond compatriot.

"May I help you?" he asked politely.

"Yes," Pete replied. "I want to file a claim and a plan of salvage on a monocar."

"I see. If you'll give me the details, I'll jot down the primary report. A monocar, you say?"

"Yes. I answered a call for help and located the car

95

just off the Badlands."

"You can give me an exact location later. What was your procedure?"

"I approached the car and found it to be damaged from a collision. Its air had been lost and the steering jets were so badly damaged it was out of control."

"The car was occupied?"

"Yes. A girl was inside. Her name is Jane Barry."

That meant nothing to the clerk and Pete automatically concluded he had never seen Jane or it would have meant something.

"What did you do?"

"I grappled onto the car and returned it to its home port."

"The girl remained in the craft during the trip?"

"Yes."

The clerk looked up from his jottings. "The rules on salvage are quite detailed. Let me get the manual."

"Do that."

The clerk took a heavy volume from under the counter and began thumbing through the pages. Pete knew what the book contained. It listed spaceships, their every component, and their every function. There were listings of ships by size, classification and origin; ships by tonnage, speed, and method of propulsion; ships by content subdivided into live and inanimate; the inanimate cut down into animal, vegetable, or mineral, each heading again reduced to classifications that filled ten pages; the live alternative was under two main heads: Human and Subhuman, these two heads going blithely on for another fifty pages.

In short, the Guide on Salvage Classifications was complete.

"I assume," the clerk said after studying the Procedure Rules section of the guidebook, "that your reason for returning to the car's home port was to deliver the girl into safety."

"Exactly," Pete agreed.

"Otherwise, you would have taken possession of the car and brought it to our depot for evaluation."

"That's just what I would have done."

"But so long as the car was delivered into its home port it could not have been legally moved unless the owner recognized your claim and settled it by delivering the car into your ownership."

"That was the situation."

"I gather, then, that there was disagreement as to the just amount of the salvage claim."

"Oh, yes," Pete assured him. "There was a big disagreement on that point."

The clerk looked up in complete disinterest. "And your claim was . . . ?"

"Transfer of ownership of the car in the state of disrepair that I found it."

"Quite harsh," the clerk murmured.

"It's legal," Pete replied.

"Were salvage costs discussed before you moved the car?"

"They weren't even mentioned."

"Did the occupant have access to other sources of help?"

"I got the call over the Emergency Band. I assume

others heard it."

"Then your action appears to be legal. I'll give you a salvage order." He began filling in a form and added, "Of course the other party does not have to honor this claim. But if it is not honored, the party must appear at this office within two days to file formal objections. Then the case goes before a referee."

"I understand," Pete said. He took his form and left the office.

Rachel Barry stared in hurt amazement. The two younger Barrys gaped, round-eyed, at Pete. But Jane was neither stunned nor frozen.

"Are you out of your mind?" she cried.

Pete had moored onto the *Snapdragon*, had been admitted into the weird interior of the ship, and had formally presented his salvage claim.

"No," he said, briskly. "I'm not out of my mind. I'm handing you a perfectly legal claim for services rendered."

99

"You mean," Rachel Barry wailed, "that you're taking our monocar in payment for doing a small, neighborly favor?"

"The salvage classifications specify otherwise. It states in the guidebook—"

"I don't care what it states!" Jane protested. "You're trying to steal my car and I won't let you do it."

"You have a legal right to enter a protest."

"How could you do a thing like this?" Rachel pleaded. "You're a nice boy. Or I thought you were. But you're only a—a thief."

"Speaking of thieves," Pete said, "I guess I'm in good company." He'd turned his eyes on Jane now, and his face was grim. "Did you go with your Uncle Homer to steal my claim or did he do it by himself?"

"What are you talking about?"

"I'm talking about a filing early this morning on the claim I located yesterday just before I came to your rescue. Which of your sisters took the filled-in form out of my pocket while they were climbing all over me?"

The big, round eyes of the younger Barrys got bigger and rounder. "Mom," Ellen screamed. "He's calling us *thieves*."

Colleen chimed in, "We're not thieves, Mommy. We didn't steal his old paper."

Jane's face had turned icy with contempt. She spoke with sharply articulated disdain. "Oh, of course. Colleen stole it. She's very sharp for her age. A mere child, but she understands every detail of a claim form and senses values instinctively. After you left she got into our disabled monocar and—"

"Cut it out!" Pete snapped. "I lost the form and this was the only place it could have happened. As I was leaving, your Uncle Homer arrived. This morning he filed a claim on my ore strike. Let's hear you talk your way out of that one."

"It's preposterous!" Rachel Barry shrieked. "You're just persecuting a helpless widow and her—"

"Mother! Stop that! Stop begging and whining. It's a lie. All of it's a great big lie!"

Pete's smile was without humor. "Now we're getting some place. I made a definite accusation and you call me a liar. I dare you to go to Parma with me and call the clerk a liar when he shows you the affidavit with Homer Deed's name on it."

"Go with him, Jane. Call his bluff. That's all it is."

"Be quiet, Mother. That would only prove Uncle Homer filed a claim this morning. It wouldn't prove it was your claim."

Pete said. "How about the original figures on the form in my handwriting? Would you dare compare it with figures Homer Deeds put down?"

"Homer was here yesterday after you left," Rachel said. "But he—"

"Mother! We're not arguing that point. Will you let me handle this?"

Rachel turned stricken eyes on her daughter and then on Pete. They were filled with sorrow. "Such a *nice* boy. It just goes to prove how a lonely widow can be fooled."

"Mother! *Will* you stop it? As for your claim, Pete Mason—if you discovered it, I assume you can find it again?"

"Of course I can find it again."

"All right, I dare you to take me there."

"To the claim? What good will that do?"

"I'm betting you can't. If you did find a strike and if Uncle Homer stole it from you and claimed it, he's probably there right now, wouldn't you say?"

"He probably is."

"But you insist on accusing a man without giving him a chance to defend himself."

Pete was puzzled, as indicated by his frown. "I don't get it—what you're driving at. Homer Deeds will get plenty of opportunity to defend himself. How could it be otherwise?"

"Sure—after you get a lot of lying witnesses together. There are plenty of miners who hate us and would jump at the chance to swear they were with you when you found the ore."

"No one was with me. And I've got no lying witnesses. The documents will speak for themselves."

Would they? In truth, Pete doubted it very much, but this was no time to show weakness.

"You're afraid to go to the claim now, though, aren't you? You're afraid to face Uncle Homer with the direct accusation."

Pete's mouth had narrowed to a grim, straight line. "Come on. It will take about two hours to get there. Can you stand being crowded into my car with me that long?"

Colleen and Ellen were wailing in chorus. "He called us thieves! He called us thieves! Uncle Homer will shoot him for that!"

"Bloodthirsty little characters, aren't they?" Pete observed coldly.

"They don't mean it," Rached assured him. "They hear things and repeat them."

"They're probably right. From what I hear about Homer Deeds, he'll probably shoot first and ask what we came for later."

Jane was moving toward the airlock. "Go ahead," she said frigidly. "Be as coarse and insulting as you wish."

"Yes," Rachel added. "Be as coarse and insulting as you wish. We're just four defenseless—"

"Don't exaggerate, Mother," Jane said in admirably controlled fury. "We're not defenseless at all. We're well able to protect our rights."

"Don't let him take our monocar," Colleen wept.

"He can't take it, darling. It's broken." She opened the lock and stood ready. "Any time, *Mister* Mason."

They climbed silently into the car, got themselves arranged as comfortably as possible and thereby became the most closely associated enemies in the Belt. As Pete lifted away, he glanced back and saw two indignant faces glued to the ports. Colleen was sticking her tongue out at him. Ellen was merely making a face.

"I'm—I'm sorry to have made your mother feel bad," Pete said. Instantly, he saw the words as a sign of weakness and wished he'd kept his mouth shut.

"You ought to be ashamed of yourself."

"Well, I'm not. I've got a perfect right to fight back when my claim's been stolen."

103

"You have yet to prove that it was stolen."

"All in due time," Pete murmured.

After that they rode in silence, and it was the strangest journey of Pete's life. The strangest and the clumsiest. He wasn't used to girls in the first place. A friendly one would have embarrassed him, crammed in this way. And Jane's hostility made it even worse. Filling the time with private meditation, Pete told himself that he wasn't mad at the Barrys. In fact he liked them. But when they stooped to taking rich ore right out of his mouth . . .

He pondered the badly mixed metaphor and wished Jane would say something. But he was darned if he'd exhibit weakness by opening the conversation himself.

As a result, there was no conversation until some time later when Jane observed, "It seems to me you're floundering all over the Belt. Do you really know where you're going?"

"I know exactly where I'm going. What do you want me to do—bang into every asteroid on the route?"

"I only want to get where we're going as soon as possible. I'm not enjoying this trip in the least."

"Are you implying that I am?"

"I merely made a statement," Jane said frostily.

"All right, you've got your wish. Look out to your right—at five o'clock. You'll see a cone-shaped asteroid. That's my claim. And the three men on it are claim-jumpers."

Involuntarily, Jane, after looking where Pete directed, tensed, laid a hand on Pete's arm, and drew it away quickly. If he'd had time to notice, this might have told Pete a great deal. But he was busy lowering the ship in and was giving the task all his attention.

Blasting operations had already begun, making it obvious that the three men were wasting no time. This, Pete realized, made sense from their point of view. Due to the notoriously slow movement of Belt law as administered by the Federation, an injunction prohibiting the removal of ore could not be served for at least a week. In that length of time, with a rich strike, three experienced miners could conceivably take out a fortune and leave the Belt with their pockets lined.

"It *is* Uncle Homer," Jane said. For the first time a small bit of uncertainty had come into her voice.

"Did you doubt it?"

Jane didn't answer and Pete realized that she'd been hoping for a mistake in identity.

The three men had stopped work and were standing motionless, watching the monocar. As its grapples tightened against the surface of the asteroid, one of them bent over. When he again came erect, he held a rifle in the crook of his arm.

"Peaceful miners," Pete commented acidly.

"They're just taking precautions. They don't know who we are."

"If Uncle Homer can't see you from here, he'd better have his eyes checked."

As he shut off the jets, Pete studied the two strangers. They wore the more elaborate helmet gear used by miners rather than the lighter oxygen equipment with the smaller headpiece. Thus their faces were pretty well hidden, and all Pete could tell for sure was that they were both big, brawny men. Uncle Homer, somewhat slighter and quicker of movement, dropped the magnetized bar he'd been working with. It rang against the surface of the asteroid and anchored itself firmly. Pete opened the bubble and started to get out of the car. Jane laid a restraining hand on his arm. He obeyed it without quite knowing why and stayed where he was.

There was a moment when everything on the asteroid alive or inanimate stood motionless. Then Uncle Homer advanced toward the car.

"What are you two doing here?"

Pete could see only his eyes. He watched them for indications of mood and attitude. They were narrowed and somewhat veiled. His abrupt tone of voice was more of a clue.

But Jane was no less abrupt. "We came here to settle something, Uncle Homer. Did you file on this claim legally?"

The eyes became a part of a deep scowl. "That's a rotten thing to say, Jane. I'm surprised at you. How else would I file on a claim?"

"That's what we're here to find out. Pete says he found this asteroid and plotted the orbit yesterday afternoon."

"That's a bald-faced lie."

"Wait a minute. He helped me home later and says he had the form in his pocket. He was wrestling with the girls and he didn't have it when he got to the claim office and he thinks one of them slipped it out of his pocket."

"Why, that's the craziest thing—"

106

The other two men were moving forward slowly. The one with the rifle stepped carefully, his body rigid and alert.

"I agree with you, Uncle Homer. Neither of the girls would do a thing like that except out of curiosity, maybe, and then they'd show it to Pete and ask him what it was."

"You let him make a charge like that and didn't—"

Jane wasn't letting him finish his sentences. She was commanding the situation, but this margin of advantage was dubious at best.

"Never mind that. As I said, the girls didn't take the form. But it might have dropped out of his pocket."

"You're talking in riddles!"

The retort meant nothing so far as Pete could see and he didn't think it was meant to. Homer Deeds, his scowl deepening, was grabbing words at random.

"I'm making complete sense," Jane retorted. "I'm saying the form might have been dropped. None of us found it or we would have returned it to Pete. But you came into the ship right after he left."

There was another of those motionless pauses in which the people acting out this tableau could have been part of the asteroid they were anchored to. Then Jane asked the next question.

"Did you pick up the form, Uncle Homer? Did you pick it up and put it into your pocket and use it to file on Pete's claim?"

"Jane! For heaven's sake!"

"You don't have to get excited, Uncle Homer. Just answer the question. A simple yes or no will do."

The man with the rifle had been moving forward.

107

He was holding the weapon at a more threatening angle now.

"What is this?" he demanded. His voice was deep and quiet. There was a calm, deadly quality about it.

"We're trying to get at the truth," Jane said.

"Possession is the proof," the man replied. "This claim is legally filed."

"That's right," Uncle Homer echoed in a weaker, more sullen voice. "I'm surprised at you, Jane. Coming out here and bringing him with you. You know how it is with us. Everybody is down on the Barrys. We've got to stick together."

"She's got to stick," the man with the rifle said. "What else can she do?"

Uncle Homer turned and glanced uncertainly at the man, then looked back at Jane. "Honey, how would you like to have everything you ever wanted?"

"Uncle Homer, I asked you a question. All I want you to do is tell me the truth. Did you steal this claim?"

"Listen here, Deeds. This is no time to lose your nerve. The girl's got to play it our way. If I've got it figured right, the kid's got all the papers on him. Nobody can connect him with the claim if he's not around to push his complaint. He has an accident . . ."

Pete saw Uncle Homer's eyes harden. He didn't have the courage to commit murder himself, but with the triggerman's recklessness to lean on, he would go along with it.

Pete sat frozen. This was incredible. He'd heard stories of men desperate enough to murder for a rich claim, but he'd never believed them, because no proof had ever been found. The Asteroid Belt was vast—most of it uncharted. Millions of miles of ever-moving, ever-restless rock clusters, where finding a body was next to impossible.

"Let's quit jabbering and get it over with," the third man said. It was the first time he'd spoken and now it appeared that he was the leader. Without hesitation, the other man brought up his rifle.

Left on his own, Pete would have been dead within the next three seconds. But he was not without an ally. As the rifle began moving upward, Jane jammed her foot down on the switch that controlled the movement of the bubble. It snapped into place. The rifle cracked simultaneously and a slug scratched the thick, bullet-proof surface of the bubble and angled down against the rock of the asteroid.

Another slug followed it; then another, and Pete heard Jane shrieking in his ear. "Move it! Don't sit there! Do you want to get killed?"

Uncle Homer was coming closer. With Pete's possible escape looming as a danger to him, he became more decisive. Had he been able to bring his weight to bear, he might have held the car back long enough for the other two men to come to his aid. Then it would have been a simple matter to prevent its take-off and pry the bubble away with the tools they had available.

But Pete cut off the magnetic grapple and hit the jet switch with the same motion and the monocar shot upward, Uncle Homer's hand scraping the sides as it pulled away from him.

The man with the rifle was still firing, pouring slugs after the car with frantic haste. They smashed against the underplating of the car, but construction heavy enough to stand against Belt conditions stood also against a rifle of the caliber that threw the slugs.

As they arced away from the asteroid, the third man was already moving toward the scout car they had used to pirate the claim.

"They'll come after us," Jane said. "They'll have to. And that scout's bigger and faster than we are. Open up your jets! Gain whatever distance you can."

"Thanks—thanks for saving my life," Pete mumbled as he peered backward and saw the three men climbing into the scout.

"Shut up and move this go-cart! Your life isn't saved yet by any means."

They sat silent now as Pete opened the jets wide and took chance after chance with possible collision in order to maintain the speed. The initial shock over, Pete's mind was beginning to work again. He was surprised at his own lack of fear even as he looked back and saw the scout already in space, circling to locate the still visible monocar.

"You're right about the speed difference. They'll run us down in ten minutes."

"If we dodge and twist—"

"No. We can't run, so we've got to hide. I think I can make the Badlands before they catch us. In there we'll have a chance."

Jane relinquished leadership, her silence an acknowledgment of this.

"Hang on for possible collision," Pete ordered. "I've

got to cut across the stream."

"Be careful," Jane whispered. And reverting from strong savior to the fragile female, she closed her eyes and put her face against Pete's shoulder.

The agile, highly responsive monocar did insane loops and turns as Pete kept changing course to avoid the asteroid stream that would have casually crushed them and gone on its way undisturbed. Once a lumbering asteroid twice the size of the monocar hit the bubble. But the crushing surface was smooth rather than murderously jagged, and the car bounced away to roll over several times before it balanced off. As they approached the edge of the Badlands, Pete guessed wrong and blundered into a swarm of fist-sized asteroids that smashed savagely against the little car's plates. But again, providentially, none of them were large enough nor was there a differential in speed great enough to allow damage.

Two minutes later Pete reduced speed and crept into the vast, moving field of supreme danger known as the Badlands. It was an eerie place at the point they entered, with the sunlight sifting through only in ever-changing shafts and the continual ominous sound of too-closely clustered boulders grinding each other to dust.

"They may follow us in if they're desperate enough, but now we're got an even chance," Pete said.

"Even if they don't find us, we may not get out alive." Jane, pale from reaction, lay with her head back against the rest, her eyes closed, possibly to blot out the dangerously tumbling asteroids around them.

"We'll try and hide out here for a while. Maybe

they'll give up. Then we'll cross to the other side of this cluster."

"Cross over—that's so easily said. But not quite so easily done."

Pete began searching for a likely refuge. Concentrating on the job, he was hardly aware of the silence that fell between them. Then Jane said, "I'm sorry."

"Sorry for what?"

"You were right. And finally, I had no way out. I had to admit the truth of what Uncle Homer really is."

"You had no way of knowing."

"Oh, I knew," Jane retorted bitterly. "I've known for a long time. Mother is sweet and wonderful but—well, she has a way of believing what she wants to believe. She doesn't like to think badly of anyone. And Uncle Homer is close to us. But I knew."

"You had to be loyal to your family."

"He wasn't really a part of the family. No, that wasn't the reason. Like Mother, I believed him because I wanted to. He was a pretty sorry specimen of a man, but he was all we had, and I guess the thought of the four of us being alone scared me. And Father believed in Homer, so I kept giving him the benefit of the doubt—until there weren't any doubts left."

"I want to thank you again for saving my life."

"Somehow I knew from the moment we set down that they would kill you before they'd let you go. So I was ready."

The car nosed carefully in and out among the grumbling, grinding boulders. At times, thunderous crashes were heard in the distance but none of them were close enough to send chain-reaction crashes into the area where the monocar pushed timidly forward among the great rock monsters.

There was another period of silence. Then Pete became aware of small sounds and turned to look. Jane was crying ever so quietly, her face in her hands.

Pete was frightened. He was out of his depth in coping with emotional females—and this new softness in Jane. It robbed him of the only weapon he'd ever had against her—a countering hostility.

"Here now! None of that," he said, a defensive gruffness in his voice. "You've been great. This is no time to crack up."

"I'm not cracking up. It's just that . . ."

"I know. You've had a terrific emotional shock. After years of trying hard to believe in Homer you've had to face things as they are. It's not easy to take."

"I guess that's how it is," Jane sniffled.

"But you've got to admit that it's better to know the truth."

"I hope so, because there are no doubts left now."

"Just be thankful he isn't a relative. That way, family loyalty doesn't enter into it."

"I think I'm crying for my father. He was so sweet. He was like Mother. He believed in everybody."

"He must have been a great guy."

"He—*look out.*"

Pete's glance had been momentarily on Jane. He saw her eyes widen in terror as she looked upward.

"Look out! There it is again!"

Pete jerked his head around and saw a great, dark shadow bearing swiftly down upon them.

Jane's mood and manner changed magically. In an instant, her eyes were glowing and she was an image of razor-sharp alertness.

"There it is! There it is! You thought I was crazy! Now what have you got to say?"

She was clutching his arm and Pete shook her off. "Let go of me! That thing's trying to crush us."

That impression was inescapable. It was definitely a huge spaceship of some sort. At first glance it looked to possess a grotesque, lopsided nose of fantastic proportions. Then Pete saw that the protuberance wasn't a nose at all. It was an asteroid against which the ship was lodged—fusion of some sort following a crash, he surmised.

But he had little time to ponder this weird phenomenon because the vast elongated bulk of the ship was smashing directly down upon the monocar. Without time to select a path, Pete jetted the car into a sharp forty-five-degree horizontal turn and slithered out from under the monster with the hull scarcely three feet away.

The maneuver could have driven him head-on into an asteroid, but he found the way clear. He jetted to the edge of a cluster well beyond range of the flailing hull and eased to a halt. Turning the car and setting his speed at drift, silently they looked back at the thing that had almost killed them.

"It's—it's impossible!" Pete babbled. "What kind of a ship is it? How did it get in here?"

"The getting here isn't too hard to figure out," Jane said. "It drifted in—pushed its way through because it's bigger than anything it encountered."

"But what pilot in his right mind would permit such a thing?"

"It doesn't look to me as though there's anyone alive inside. It's just drifting."

"Then where did they go?"

"How would I know?" Jane snapped, and if Pete had been in the mood to notice, he would have concluded that Jane was her snappish, disagreeable self again.

But his attention was elsewhere "There's something

funny about that ship," he said.

"That's certainly the understatement of the day."

"I mean something really funny. Something more than just a strange ship adrift in the Badlands. It tried to kill us."

"What's odd about that? You moved right in under it."

"Do you notice anything strange about this layout?"

"What do you mean?"

"This is a pretty solid area of the Badlands. It's thick with drifting asteroids. Yet there's an empty pocket around that ship. Not a rock within range of it."

"Pure coincidence?"

"I'm not so sure. I'll swear that wasn't a casual drift that almost got us. It was controlled movement."

"You're crazy. The ship came back to balance and now it's just running along with the drift."

"I'm not blind," Pete grumbled. "I can see what it's doing. But—wait a minute. Hold on tight."

"What are you going to do?"

"I'm going to try something."

"Don't be stupid! You'll get us killed yet."

"I don't think so."

"That's comforting, but I'd like you to be positive before you make any moves."

Pete ignored her as he made the move he had in mind. Tensed for an instant reaction, he jetted the car slowly forward into the open space around the ship. Nothing happened. They moved closer. Then, as they came inside the arc the ship was capable of while swinging with its imprisoned nose as a fulcrum, there was definite movement.

116

The hull shuddered and swung in their direction.

"Did you see that?"

Pete cut sharply to the right, drew a tight arc of his own, and went back to his drifting spot. From this point of safety they watched the giant swing around until it passed through the position they had lately occupied. Then its apparent drift ceased, and it swung back into a straight line with the drift of the stream.

"What did you prove?" Jane asked innocently.

"Didn't you *see* what I proved?"

"Just that it's easy to get killed in here."

"That ship lashed out at us."

"And you laughed at me for calling it a live thing. Actually, all you did was make a move coincident with a magnetic drift-swing."

Pete smiled, "I'm glad you're getting your feet back on the ground."

"That sounds funny—out here."

"I was speaking figuratively."

"Look—will you stop pushing our luck? We've brushed close to death seven distinct times that I recall, and now—"

Pete ignored her as he pushed carefully back into the cluster behind them. Safely inside, he selected an asteroid about half the size of the monocar and put his nose gently against it. Then he pushed the asteroid slowly out into the open.

When he had it clear of the cluster, he put more power to the jets and forced the big rock into an intermediate arc that would carry it within range of the spaceship's lateral swing.

"Now watch."

"What am I supposed to see?"

Pete pointed. "That!"

As though the approach of the asteroid constituted a signal, the hull of the ship began to arc around on its rock fulcrum. At one point, both Pete and Jane gasped as the ship elevated its swing with a definitely artificial upward jerk. Thus, when its plates hit the approaching asteroid, it was with a dead-center contact that reversed the asteroid's course and sent it spinning back into the cluster.

"All right," Pete said grimly. "Was that natural magnetic drift?"

"It knocked the asteroid back into the cluster!"

"Exactly. And what does that prove?"

Jane smiled with a touch of mockery. "I'm all ears, teacher. What *does* it prove?"

"A cybernetic brain."

"Well, aren't you the clever one? A ship with a cybernetic brain patterned to batting asteroids around the Belt. A rather expensive child's toy, I'd say."

"If you're so blasted smart, figure out your own riddles," Pete snapped. "I'd say it's some sort of a defense mechanism. A pilotless ship is vulnerable. It repels boarders or at least makes boarding difficult. And it can clear its own path if necessary."

Happy at having needled Pete sucessfully, Jane was all apology. "I'm sorry. I didn't know you were so touchy. What will we do now?"

Pete glanced at her and found her expression so guileless and trusting that he felt guilty at being annoyed. "I think we ought to try and board her. I think she's a derelict."

"What makes you think that?"

"Because we get no signal. We might get shot to pieces or welcomed with open arms, but we certainly wouldn't be ignored by a live ship."

"That reminds me," Jane said. "I want to call home."

Passing quickly through the emergency band, Jane put the *Snapdragon*'s call letters on the public channel and a few moments later Rachel Barry's plaintive voice came in. "Jane! You poor child! What are they doing to you now?"

"Nothing, Mother, but a lot has happened."

"Can we keep our monocar?"

Jane looked blank for a moment. So much had happened that she'd forgotten about Pete's salvage threat. "Yes, Mother—I mean, no—well, maybe." Jane looked appealingly at Pete. He was no help. "An awful lot has happened, Mother."

"Then *tell* me, child. Did that awful Pete Mason apologize to Uncle Homer for the things he said?"

"No, Mother. I can't tell you about it now. It was the other way."

"Uncle Homer apologized to—"

"No. He tried to kill him."

"Jane! You aren't making sense. Who tried to kill whom?"

"Mother, this is a public channel. I'll tell you later. Right now we're in the Badlands. We found a strange ship and—" Jane stopped, becoming quite confused herself. "Mother, I'll tell you all about it when we get back."

"When will that be?"

"I don't know. I've got to cut out. Uncle Homer

might get a fix on us if he's listening."

"Why should he want to do that? Jane! What's going on?"

"Mother, I've got to cut out! I'll call you later."

Jane snapped the switch. "I guess I shouldn't have called," she said. "Mother will worry her head off now."

Pete wasn't paying any attention. He was studying the mysterious derelict that now hung motionless in the stream with its nose glued to the huge, jagged asteroid.

"I'm going to try to grapple on," he said.

"But you just saw what happens when—"

"It would have to really whip around to throw us off with our magnets on full. If it starts shaking our teeth loose, we'll let go."

"It certainly ought to be fun," Jane said dubiously.

"Fun or not, there's something you're overlooking."

"If you're referring to salvage possibilities, I'm way ahead of you. If that ship is a derelict it could make the Barrys rich."

"What about the Masons?"

"Oh, we'd be generous and declare you in."

"Well, thanks a pile!"

Pete wasn't as annoyed as he sounded. He thought it probable that Jane was deliberately forcing the light, bantering mood. Her moment of truth relative to Uncle Homer had hit her hard. He admired the about-face courage she was showing.

"Here goes," he said. "I'm going in fast so we can clamp on before she starts swinging."

"Good luck—good luck to both of us—but how do

you know her reaction potential? You saw lazy swings against slow-moving objects."

"A ship that big can't react sharply enough to be dangerous."

"Just for the sake of argument," Jane said, "I'll bet it can."

Pete gauged his angle visually and jammed down on the jet switch. "Women!" he muttered disdainfully.

A few moments later, after a monstrous swish of suddenly hurled metal brushed their grapplers, they were whirling end-over-end toward a wall of clustered asteroids.

Pete clawed desperately at the controls and reversed to a halt with a jagged shaft of rock just ready to ram in through the bubble. With the car hanging on balance, they untangled themselves. Jane pushed her hair out of her eyes and said, "You're very good. Your reflexes and your skill saved our lives."

"Thank you."

"But of course that was after your stupidity put us in danger."

Pete neglected to thank Jane for that. He stared at the ship as it settled back into its trough behind the asteroid. "That does it. We can't board the idiotic tub!"

"Oh, I wouldn't say that," Jane replied airily.

"What's your idea?"

"If I was in charge I'd go around in front and ease the car over the asteroid. The brain's got a time-span quotient or it would still be trying to shake off the asteroid its nose is fused to. If we came in from that side . . ."

Pete was staring, still expressionless, at the weird ship.

"All right!" Jane exploded. "It's only a mechanical brain. Its deductive abilities are limited to its patterns. Come in from the front and you might fool the crazy thing!"

"I didn't say it wasn't a good idea," Pete snapped.

"Thanks for the credit."

Pete did not reply as he pointed the car along the wall of the open circle and moved around in front of the asteroid that had captured the spaceship. He nosed up over its jagged surface and inched toward the spot where the collision fusion had melted the craft and the asteroid together.

"That ship certainly took a sweet punch in the nose," he muttered.

The fusion area—metal and lava run together—was at least ten feet wide.

"It doesn't make sense," Jane said. "How could a ship and an asteroid fuse that way? One of them should have been smashed to dust."

"The only way it could have happened seems impossible."

"What way?"

"As I see it, the collision occurred out in space. Either the ship or the asteroid was revolving at a high rate of speed at the time of contact. Two coincident motions would have been necessary."

"You mean high-speed trajectory and rotation at the same time."

"That's right. But how could such a situation have been brought about?"

"I'd say an asteroid. Knocked off a larger body, it could have a forward-spinning motion in the same direction as its trajectory!"

"And the new trajectory formed by the collision brought the ship and the asteroid into the Badlands."

"Well, no pilot in his right mind would have brought it here, that's for sure," Jane said.

Pete was watching the ship as though he expected it to grow a fist and knock him back where he'd come from. "We seem to be getting away with it," he said cautiously.

"The brain can't differentiate us from the asteroid it's accepted."

"Maybe it would be smart if we grappled onto the fusion area. Then I'll walk onto the hull and hang on by my boots."

Jane was doubtful now. "I don't know. Maybe we ought to go for help."

"And split the salvage?"

"Your father and Betcha—"

"No," Pete said firmly. "We've got to find out more about this tub. I think the brain would accept established contact—a magnetic grip—because it accepted the fused asteroid."

"We'll both go."

"You stay here. You'll have to pick me up if I get thrown off."

They activated their heat and air equipment, and Pete opened the bubble and crawled out of the car. He grappled to the fused surface and then began moving forward. Jane watched tensely from the car as he came to the edge of the fusion and stepped across.

Nothing happened. He moved his other foot forward. There was no reaction from the ship. Slowly, then with increasing confidence, he moved out onto the massive hull and turned to motion Jane toward him. A few moments later, she, too, was crossing the fusion area and grappling to the hull with her magnetic boots. Pete waited for her and as she came close he noted the confused and questioning look on her face.

"Do you feel what I feel?" she asked.

"As though you're sinking into something soft?"

"Yes—as though we haven't got any footing. I have to keep looking down to be sure I'm not sinking in."

Intrigued, they both squatted down to check further into their joint reaction. Pete laid his gloved hand flat on the dull, sheenless metal of the hull. He stared at his hand for a few moments and then looked up at Jane.

"It's weird. My sense of touch tells me I'm sinking in up to my elbow. But my eyes say my hand is lying on a hard surface. I don't know which to believe."

"There's something very weird about this hull—this metal."

"Your perception astounds me," Pete said dryly.

Jane refused to be baited. "I think the sinking-in phenomenon is side effect. This is a highly specialized metal with specifics and capabilities beyond our knowledge." She raised her eyes. There was awe and a certain fright in them. "This ship wasn't built in our system."

Pete was surprised. "You sound like an upper classman in an engineering school."

"Maybe I'm not very smart, but I was with my father a lot. He was a brilliant man. I couldn't help learning a little about spaceships."

Unaware of how much that *little* was going to turn out to be, Pete came to his feet and looked about helplessly. "Well, at least the tub isn't throwing us off."

"How did you plan to get inside? No matter how far we sink, we're still out here."

"I assumed that if the ship is empty it had been abandoned. In that case, there should be an open hatch someplace. If not, maybe I can climb in through a jet tube."

"Did you see any while she was swinging her tail around?"

"No, as a matter of fact, I didn't."

"Neither did I."

"Then we'd better start hunting. We're probably on borrowed time."

"What do you mean?"

"If Homer Deeds and his two friends aren't smart enough to track us here, it would be a big surprise to me."

Pete glanced around at the circular walls of the ominous pocket they were in; a pocket formed in a clump of asteroids jammed together and moving as a single body.

"Another thing—if an asteroid blunders into range and activates this tub's crazy responses, we'll get thrown into next week."

At that moment a new and ominous grinding of rock on rock was telegraphed through the asteroids across the Badlands.

"How far away was that?" Jane asked.

"I don't know, but it's a lot too close. Let's hurry."

As they moved—as though walking through molasses—toward the ship's tail, the same thought was in both their minds. They'd been rather proud of the victory they'd achieved in putting their boots to the hull.

But they seemed to have merely won their way into greater trouble.

"It doesn't look like a jet to me," Jane said.

"Maybe it's just a steering tube, but it's still a hole," Pete replied. "I'm going in."

"And leave me out here all alone?"

This wail from Jane, Pete thought, was refreshing after a fashion—a definitely feminine reaction from a girl who could be very unfeminine a great deal of the time.

"Well, we can't squeeze in together, and until we find out the score, it's safer out here than in there."

Jane watched as Pete eased himself into the narrow,

circular opening feet-first. A few moments later he pushed his head out.

"It isn't a jet or a steering tube. It's an escape hatch of some kind. Come on."

Jane lost no time and Pete pulled her into a small chamber with enough room for three or four people to stand comfortably. Jane pointed to the inner wall.

"That's the outer seal of the airlock, but how do we open it?"

Pete ran his hands over the surface of the inner wall. Then he looked at Jane strangely, took off his gloves, and repeated the examination.

"It's warm!"

Jane frowned. "That doesn't make sense!" She took off her own gloves and touched the wall and her expression changed. Perhaps it didn't make sense but nonetheless the wall was a hundred degrees warmer than the unchanging temperature of the Belt.

"Pete, I'm scared."

"So am I, but—"

"There's too much here that contradicts logic. In the first place, this ship could easily be a thousand years old. The pittings on the hull alone indicate great age and passage through the kind of bombardments we just don't get in the System. Any sort of creature we find inside would have to have an incredible life span. That and other things give us ample reason to believe the ship is an ancient, lifeless derelict. But its walls are warm!"

"Don't panic," Pete advised. "Just keep on using your precious logic. There must be something inside that can create heat indefinitely."

"A ship powered by fusionable material with a half-life of more than a thousand years?"

"Exactly."

"But atomic fusion isn't the method here. Where are the jets?"

"Let's not turn this into a debating society or there's going to be a gun poked in at us and it won't matter. I'm wondering how to crack that outer air seal."

"That shouldn't be too difficult," Jane said. "The control of the hatches and the ports must be centered in the cybernetic brain."

"Sure, but it didn't open on entry. So what's the signal?"

"There shouldn't have to be any. This is a space-ship, not a bank vault." Jane tapped on the panel of the air seal. Nothing happened.

"Looks as though the brain isn't receiving today," Pete said.

"Pressure might be the key," Jane said. She put both hands on the seal and pressed her weight against it.

The seal opened.

"Sure," Pete said. "The seal is controlled by a memory bank adjusted to pressure."

"All it takes," Jane said with understandable smugness, "is a little common sense."

Pete followed her into a larger chamber and the door closed behind them. In a moment they could hear air hissing in. At the same time a narrow panel over their head began to glow. It reached apparent capacity quickly, throwing a faint light into the chamber.

"Pretty stingy with the electric power," Pete said.

"If you were a light panel you'd be pretty feeble too, after a thousand years," Jane said.

"You seem to be pretty sure of your time span."

Jane ignored his doubt. "This ship hasn't been in out of the void long, either."

"Of course not. The atmosphere in the Belt is too thin to sustain life, but it would be enough to rust that seal tight in, say a hundred years."

Jane was a little disappointed at having the point of her observation snatched away. "Aren't we smart, though," she said. Then, before Pete could think of an answer, the inner seal opened and the bowels of the strange and frightening ship were open to them.

The light was a little brighter inside and a metal stairway led downward.

"She's got a magnetic field of her own," Pete said.

Jane didn't comment on the observation. Pete had stated the obvious. Even with their boots turned off, they could move by their own weight. The strength of the field was proven by the fact that the ship sat horizontal. The magnetic drift of her asteroid captor was not enough to turn her from an even keel.

Pete went down the stairs. Jane followed. Twenty feet down, a narrow companionway leveled off, leading them forward. "We're walking on the keel plate," Pete said. "There are no escapeways from stern to prow."

"Not necessarily strange," Jane replied. "We agreed that this ship wasn't designed in the System."

"At least not in the Inner System. It could have come from Jupiter."

His observation was based on a point of history. It

was accepted as fact that space explorers from Jupiter and perhaps beyond had penetrated the Inner System. Why they had never followed through was a mystery couched in many theories. The most universally accepted one was that a deterioration in Outer System civilization had destroyed the technology that made space travel possible.

But neither Jane nor Pete were greatly interested in history at the moment. The long, brooding companionway held greater fascination. As they approached the forward end, Jane stopped suddenly and grasped Pete's arm. There was a rapt look on her face.

"Can't you feel it?"

"Feel what?"

"I don't know. A presence. An intelligence. I can't explain it."

If she expected a cynical rebuff from Pete, he certainly must have surprised her with his reply.

"I think you're very lucky."

"Please don't laugh at me."

"I'm not laughing. A first-year psychology student in this day and age knows the value of a highly developed sixth sense. It has many names. Extra-sensory perception—high-vibratory sensitivity—electro-intelligence affinity. But it adds up to the same thing—conscious receptivity at levels above the human norm."

Jane blinked. She was on the verge of a defensively cynical reply herself, but then she simply said, "Are you sure archeology is your field?"

He ignored the question. "You certainly know what's happening to you, don't you?"

131

"I'm not sure."

"You're mentally picking up the synthetic thought patterns that are coming out of the memory of the cybernetic brain controlling this ship."

Jane stared blankly and Pete shot a quick question. "Where is the unit?"

Jane replied instantly, without thought. She pointed upward and forward. "It's in the control room just behind the nose of the ship."

"Why wasn't it smashed when the ship hit the asteroid?"

"Because it's fifty feet back—behind a three-foot crash wall of . . ."

"Of what?"

Jane shook her head and then passed a hand across her brow. "I don't know! I . . . a . . ."

"But *almost* knew—you almost read the name of the material out of the brain's thought patterns. The brain knows—it was told."

Jane's eyes showed disbelief but she did not contradict Pete. She pulled her head piece down. "You don't have to wear that thing. There's plenty of air in here."

Pete grinned. "Which proves something else."

"What?"

"That this ship came from an oxygen breathing world."

Jane's eyes widened. "Then it can't be Jupiterian. It had to come from so far out—"

"From so far out that it couldn't have possibly reached our system."

"But it's here."

"It's here," Pete said grimly. "Let's take a look at the brain . . ."

Jane led the way, moving forward as confidently as though this were the bowels of the *Snapdragon*. She climbed the stairs at the end of the companionway and went through a doorway that led to a higher one running in the same direction. There, she turned forward and opened another door.

"It's in there."

The cabin was singularly bare. Some twenty feet square, its walls were of a bright metal and there was a control panel on the forward wall.

In the center of the cabin, surrounded by a waist-railing, a slim pedestal reared out of the floor supporting a bright metal globe with a ten-foot diameter.

"That's it," Jane said. "Can you hear the hum?"

"No."

"I can. It's very faint. Not even like a sound."

"Your receptions are fine enough to record it."

"What is it?"

"The synthetic thought stuff coming from the memory banks of the thing. I read a book of experiments on cybernetics at school. If you're highly sensitive, you should translate what comes to you as a mood."

"I think it's sick," Jane said.

Pete regarded her in silence. He was struck by the change in her. The subtle forces she was encountering had temporarily submerged and blanketed her extrovert personality pattern.

What she'd just said dawned on her and she looked frightened. "Pete! That's crazy. What's wrong with me? Calling a machine sick!"

133

"There's nothing crazy about that. The unit is out of order. It's the same thing."

"You mean it's talking to me?"

"Of course not. You're merely interpreting emotionally because it's the only way you can express what's coming to you. Let's forget the brain for a while and do a little checking."

Jane followed Pete forward where they studied the control panel. "There are a few things to be learned here," he said grimly.

"The symbols on the dials. What kind of a language is that?"

"The closest thing I've seen to them are the ancient Earth languages. Egyptian—Sanskrit—maybe even ancient Chinese. It would take real scholars to make them out. But there's something else of interest here."

"What, Pete?"

"A couple of things, so we'll take them one at a time. When we were outside, did you see any ports on this ship?"

"No."

"Then I guess you haven't noticed—we can see out."

"Pete! You're crazy!"

"Am I? Face the bulkhead squarely and look straight ahead of you. What do you see?"

Jane obeyed. Her eyes widened in amazement. After staring for a few moments, she turned her gaze on Pete. "I can see the rocks out in the Belt—out in the Badlands!"

"You're looking out through a round port."

"But it's impossible."

"It's some kind of strange refraction. I noticed it when we walked forward. As you move along the bulkhead, the window goes with you. At right angles to the eye the plates of this ship are transparent. Shift the angle about ten degrees in any direction and the visibility ceases."

Phenomena following after each other so rapidly had dazed Jane. "There's one thing I noticed all by myself," she said. "That soft, muddy sensation when you walk—it's not on the inside. Everything is solid here. Even the inner sides of the plates."

"You're right! I've been so busy looking at other things I hadn't noticed. Then the characteristics of the metal that produce that effect are only on the outside."

"What do you suppose it means?"

"I don't know—the characteristics were brought out through know-how we're unfamiliar with. I'm sure the outer softness is a phenomenon involved in the greater durability of the metal. At least that makes sense."

Again Jane seized Pete's arm. She moved close to him and looked into his face and when she spoke it was in a whisper. "Pete. It turned! The brain! I'm scared."

Pete looked blankly at the big metal globe. "What do you mean it turned?"

"It can turn on that pedestal. And it did turn—as though it's listening to us."

"But you're facing away from it and there was no sound . . . how . . . ?"

"I don't care where I'm facing. The darn thing knows we're here and I want to get out."

Pete shrugged. "That's not so strange. It knows when an asteroid comes too close, so why shouldn't it know when we're standing right next to it?"

Jane stood close, needing the comfort of feeling Pete near her. "I don't like it here. Let's go someplace else."

"All right," he said cheerfully. "We'll explore. But don't start letting that cybernetic unit scare you. You're going to have to help it get well."

"Pete! Stop being silly."

"I'm not being silly. There has to be a self-repairing component in a unit that brought this ship from far outer space. It knows what's wrong with it."

"Why does there have to be? The technicians and the crew would make repairs."

"Maybe," Pete said cryptically. "Let's see what's aft at this level."

They went back into the companionway and chose the first of two doors that were offered. It opened on a cabin about half the size of the one that housed the brain. It was of the same shining metal and was filled with black rectangular boxes piled row on row in neat stacks.

"The memory banks," Pete said.

Jane gasped. "All those? The brain must be able to remember things back to the dawn of time!"

"No, it was given just enough to go where it was supposed to and find its way back."

Jane clung to his arms as she stared at the cabin's contents. "I don't like it here. Let's get out."

"Are the thought emanations hostile?"

"No . . . no . . ." Jane's nose wrinkled and her brow

136

furrowed. "It has to sound idiotic but I get a feeling that it's crying."

"Not idiotic at all. That could be the emotional translation of its own synthetic thought reactions to its breakdown. Let's see what's in the next cabin."

It was a vast enclosure going up to the apex of the hull plates.

"Storage," Pete said. "All those boxes. They must contain food and supplies for the trip."

"But none of them have been used. This hold is jammed full."

"Maybe there are other supply holds."

There were. Hold after hold reaching back to the stern of the ship—six in all—three filled to capacity and three completely empty.

The farther they went from the cybernetic brain up front, the brighter Jane's mood became. When they reached the tail, her eyes were bright and her face glowed.

"Pete! We're rich! Do you realize that? This ship is priceless! And it's all ours—for salvage."

"I hope so."

"What do you mean? It *is* ours."

"We haven't filed our salvage plan yet. Maybe—"

He stopped as he caught the expression on Jane's face. She was staring out through the hull plate. She pointed. "A monocar!"

"Homer Deeds!" Pete said automatically.

"No. It's Mother and the girls!"

"That's ridiculous!" Pete snapped. "You're seeing things!"

He searched the wall of the pocket outside as Jane

137

snapped the switch on her head piece radio unit.

"Mother! What are you doing out there? Why aren't you home in the *Snapdragon?*"

Then Pete saw them—jammed together in the crippled car he'd towed home after rescuing Jane. He snapped on his own unit and heard Rachel Barry's cheerful voice.

"We were worried about you. So we got a fix and came hunting. Are you all right, dear?"

"How did you get here in that car without killing yourself?" Pete demanded.

"Oh, it works all right. You just have to keep righting it and pulling it back on course."

"It goes end-over-end all the time," Colleen wailed.

"What are you doing in that funny-looking ship?" Ellen asked.

The car came looping out into the open area. Jane brought a quick hand to her mouth. "Mother! Go back! Go back in among the rocks and wait there. This ship will smash you to pieces!"

"The ship will smash us? What kind of nonsense are you talking, dear? Open the hatch and let us in."

The next fifteen minutes was frantic. First, Pete and Jane watched in horror as Rachel Barry urged the balky monocar out into the area the space ship was keeping clear.

"Mother! Go back! Go back!" Jane screamed.

Rachel Barry was puzzled. "What's wrong with you, child? Why shouldn't we come aboard?"

"The ship will slug you!" Pete yelled.

"Why, I never heard of such nonsense!"

"Go back!"

It was too late even if the stubborn mother of the Barry brood had chosen to listen. The spaceship had already taken aim with its tail and was swinging murderously.

As they watched through the windows and saw the outer world streak by, Jane and Pete looked at each other in consternation. But they had no time to comment on what had astounded them, because Rachel's voice came in a moment later.

"This pesky car! It does what it pleases."

"They weren't hit!" Jane marveled.

Another moment and the monocar came back into view and Pete realized what had happened. "The car did a backflip over the ship and went back where it came from! The ship missed it!"

"Mother! Stay where you are!" Jane shouted. We'll come out and get you."

"Well, all right. I can't seem to get the grapples down on the hull."

"I'll go," Pete said. "I've got a hand jet in my car."

"Pete's coming to guide you in," Jane said.

Pete hurried away and a few minutes later, Jane saw him through the transparent plate, pushing his way toward the crippled car. Once there, he grasped the landing grid bar in one hand, pointed the activated hand jet rearward, and pulled the car slowly along the wall of the cluster toward the fused prow of the ship.

As he moved beyond range of her vision, Jane went to the companionway and ran back to the air lock, where she was waiting when her family entered.

Colleen's eyes were round with wonder. "This is going to be fun!" she announced.

The elder of the two Barrys, Ellen, was somewhat more reserved. "When we walked along the hull it was like wading in rock dust," she said.

"Yes," Rachel agreed. "What sort of a ship is this, Jane?"

"We don't know, Mother, but it's a salvage price that will make us all rich—that's for sure."

"How did you ever find it, child?"

Jane looked suddenly tired, and Pete knew the incident with Homer Deeds and his two friends had come to mind; that and the realization that she would have to tell her mother the truth about the man they had treated as one of the family.

"It's a long story, Mother. Right now Pete and I have to figure out how to get this ship to Parma to claim salvage."

"Where is the crew? What happened?"

"We'll find that out later. Why don't you and the girls—"

A sudden, unheralded shriek from Colleen split the air, causing Pete to jump almost out of his skin.

"What's the matter?" Jane cried.

"Omaha! We forgot Omaha. He's still in the car."

"Then it's too late," Pete said. "The bubble is open."

"That doesn't make any difference. We put his space suit on when we got here."

Pete stared. "A space suit for a cat?"

"Of course," Colleen said. "Cats have to breathe too, don't they?"

"I'll go get him," Pete said.

A space suit for a cat! Still not believing it, Pete went outside again and back to the asteroid where the two cars were grappled down. He peered into the one the Barrys had miraculously escaped death in and, sure enough, from a narrow space behind the seat, a pair of hostile eyes blazed out at him.

"Come on, you stupid feline," Pete invited.

Omaha declined. Pete looked closer and saw that the cat actually was wearing a specially built space unit! It consisted of a blanket through which Omaha's ears, legs, and tail protruded. The cat's eyes blazed out balefully at Pete over a headpiece that covered its nose.

"Come on, I said. Do you want to sit there and freeze to death?"

This seemed to make sense to Omaha. He lifted his flattened ears and deigned to jump up on the seat. Pete lifted him out of the car and, as he crossed the fused area, he found that there were tiny magnets attached to the cat's feet.

So when Omaha began to squirm, Pete set him down on the hull and pointed rearward. "Your family is back there," he muttered.

Then Pete was treated to one of the most hilarious spectacles he'd ever seen. The moment Omaha's feet touched the hull plate, he began to flounder. Pete realized instantly what was happening. The cat was also a victim of the sinking-in sensation. He looked up at Pete in consternation, and when he found no help in that direction, he began wallowing and floundering along the smooth surface of the hull.

Pete grinned. "It's like he was drunk," he chuckled.

Omaha finally achieved a kind of balance and began walking rearward, lifting his feet high in the air at each step as he marched along. A couple of times he looked back at Pete disdainfully as though he had personally arranged this ridiculous situation.

But the comedy episode ended swiftly when, from somewhere in the surrounding cluster, Pete heard a rifle crack. The sound was transmitted through the near-vacuum from a radio near its source, and Pete picked up the crack and then the *spat* of lead against the hull on his receiver.

Reacting instantly, he snatched up the cat and ran. His progress was slow and clumsy and, when a second slug was fired, he began to zigzag.

Three more shots were fired, proving beyond doubt the murderous intent behind them. But luck, lack of skill on the part of the rifleman, or Pete's zigzagging retreat, saved him from death or injury.

Safe inside the outer chamber, Pete leaned his weight against the seal. It opened with maddening slowness, and he leaped inside. There, he waited while the chamber filled, each second dragging by like an age.

When the inner seal released, Pete heard Jane speaking to her mother: "We don't dare radio for help. It would guide them straight to us."

Obviously, Jane had told her the truth about Homer Deeds and what had happened on the planetoid. But, with exasperating loyalty, Rachel Barry was still defending Homer: "It's impossible! Homer may be weak and maybe a little sharp in his dealings, but he isn't a murderer!"

"Well, if he isn't," Pete snapped, "he's got two killers with him, and they've tracked us here. I dodged four slugs on the way back."

"I'll talk to Homer."

"You do that," Pete said grimly. "In the meantime, I'm going topside and try to locate them."

As Pete headed toward the long companionway, he noted that the two younger girls had disappeared, that Rachel Barry had been rooted to the floor by the developments Jane had passed on to her, and that Omaha was yowling for somebody to take his suit off and relieve him of his magnets so he could walk around.

Great, Pete thought grimly. A war with salvage pirates and a family on my hands!

Jane was close behind him as he entered the first empty storage hold, the best place they'd found for outside observation.

"Are you hoping what I'm hoping?" Jane asked.

"I wouldn't be surprised. Can you spot them?"

Jane went to the center of the hold and looked straight up. "I don't see anything but rocks." She began moving, her window automatically following along overhead.

"I think they're somewhere on this side," Pete said as he walked along the bulkhead. "The shots angled in."

Jane joined him and had moved some few feet ahead when she pointed. "There they are! There's a ship in that pocket."

Pete stepped behind her and looked over her shoulder. "Sure! I can see the nose in the shadows. They're a little timid about coming out."

"They know we're in here. Maybe they're afraid we're not alone."

144

"They're too smart for that. They've sized this tub up as a derelict. But they could figure that we've found some guns."

"I'd think they'd move in fast. They must know we'll call for help. You'd better contact your father."

"Not a chance."

"What do you mean? You don't have to go back to the car. Your mobile unit will—"

"Do you think they haven't got a scrambler on us? Snap on your unit and see what happens."

Jane complied, and her face twisted as from a blow. In a sense it was a blow—an angry, snarling shaft of sound that knifed into her ears. It obviously came from a portable scrambler aboard the pirate's scout-car. Jane cut the howling racket out.

"It's against the law to scramble!" she cried.

"It's against the law to shoot people, too, but those boys are playing for keeps."

"Why can't the authorities make a fix on the sound of a scrambler?"

"This is no time for a lesson in radiotronics. Just accept my word that they can't."

Jane was shaping a reply when Pete touched her arm. "They're coming out!"

Jane's eyes brightened. She smiled. "Goody!"

"We'll see what happens."

They watched as the scout nosed out of its cave. Jane's fingernails dug into Pete's arm as the nose pointed toward the ship and the jet power was advanced.

"It's coming straight in," she breathed.

"I thought maybe they'd wonder why our ships are

grappled to the asteroid, but I guess they weren't that smart."

The hit was perfect. They were close enough to see the looks of amazement and fear of the three faces as the hull of the derelict came around and smashed the scout squarely on the nose. The bubble collapsed and the scoutcar went hurtling backward to smash in turn against the wall of an asteroid and drop down to a shelf wide enough to hold it.

"That finishes them," Jane murmured. She had buried her face in Pete's shoulder, and he knew she was thinking of Homer Deeds. She realized he deserved his fate, but she still couldn't contemplate it without tears.

"Like Mother said, he was weak."

"Don't be too sure they're finished," Pete warned. "There's heavy shielding in the back of a scoutcar and the bubble didn't smash into them."

Even as he spoke, there was movement in the smashed car and two figures emerged. A third one could be seen lying motionless in the car.

"His two friends made it. They're moving around. They don't seem to be too badly hurt."

"But they're probably plenty scared. Maybe they'll take one of the monocars and leave."

"Don't bet on it," Pete said. "They'll be slowed down for a few minutes, though, and we'd better use the time in hunting for something to defend ourselves with."

"Even if we do find weapons, we may not know how to use them."

"We can always try," Pete said. He peered around

146

the huge empty hold. "If my sense of proportions are right, we haven't covered half of this ship yet. It has odd construction. There doesn't seem to be any entrance to the lower section."

"There has to be. And we've got to find it. If we don't find some way to protect ourselves, they'll steal our salvage."

"That's not the worst. They were ready to kill me when they met me, but they wouldn't have killed you Barrys as long as Homer Deeds was with them. If he's dead and with a prize like this at stake, I don't think they'd hesitate to kill all of us."

"Do you think they really tried to kill you? Maybe they were only trying to scare—"

"Stop dreaming! This is for real. Those men would kill their own mothers for the money tied up in this derelict."

Pete stopped and suddenly snapped his fingers. "I've got to go back to the cars!"

"What for?"

"The water supply. The vapor tanks in this ship have to be bone-dry after hundreds of years. Maybe the food is still edible but we've got to have water to hold out any length of time."

"Pete! They'll be watching!"

"If I go now, while they're still groggy, I can probably make it. I'll go around the far side and they won't see me, even if they're looking, until I reach the cars."

"There *might* be water aboard."

"A million-to-one shot, and we can't use up the time in hunting."

He started aft and Jane ran to catch up with him.

Her hand stayed on his arm. "Pete, if anything happens to you . . ."

"Nothing will. Let's hurry. There's something I want to show you before I go out."

When they got to the top of the stairway that led into the air lock readyroom, Pete seized a hook and pulled it, and a heavy panel came out of the wall.

"I noticed this earlier. It's a door you can pull across the head of the stairs to block off the companionway. When I come back, I'll knock on the outer seal three times. If anyone comes in without knocking, see that everyone's out of the ready-room and close this door. It locks automatically right there. It will hold them off at least for a while."

"Pete—be careful."

"Oh, I'll be back all right. It's just that in a situation like this, we have to prepare for every possibility."

Pete went into the air lock, and the door closed behind them. Outside, he crouched and listened. He heard only the eternal grinding of the rocks in the ever-restless clusters, impressive even though muted because of the lack of atmosphere to carry the sound.

Rising, he moved down the hull to the blind side.

And met one of the two active pirates on an exploratory mission!

But the meeting was not face to face, a break for which Pete was instantly thankful. The man, the larger of the two, stood tight to the hull with his back to Pete. He seemed to be debating which way to go.

Faced with this situation in his imagination, Pete would have seen himself as panicking. But confronted with it in reality, he was surprisingly cool even as fear tightened his stomach, and found himself estimating his chances even as he laid eyes on the pirate.

They weren't very good.

The man outweighed him and, while he did not carry a rifle, he no doubt had a weapon of some kind. Pete could not possibly get back to the air lock without being seen because the man was slowly turning in his direction and would soon notice him.

Now Pete saw his weapon, a lethal tool made of unbreakable trihelium used for prying stubborn barriers. Its point and part of its blade were razor-sharp.

Once he'd set eyes on Pete, he could overtake and kill him before he could possibly get through the other air seal.

Without further thought, Pete lunged at the man. Thus, when he saw Pete coming at him in such a foolhardy fashion, he assumed the boy wasn't coming unarmed.

So he spent some crucial moments looking for the gun he was sure Pete must be carrying. Pete used that time to get close to the pirate. Then, as the deadly blade automatically lashed out, Pete dropped under it, seized the pirate's ankles, and heaved upward.

Had he failed, he would have been dead in a matter of seconds. But his desperation gave him added strength. He broke the magnetic grip that held the pirate to the hull and heaved him up and outward into space.

It was an old fighting maneuver of the asteroids; so old, the pirate hadn't thought Pete foolish enough to try it.

But the pirate had plenty of time to ponder Pete's stupidity as he shot helplessly up into space and began flailing the void with his prying tool.

Becoming instantly quite unfoolhardy, Pete turned and fled toward the air lock. The pirate wasn't going anywhere. At the worst, he would drift until he touched the surrounding cluster and then orientate himself. But if he had any measure of space skill, he would slowly work his way back down to the hull of the derelict.

As Pete disappeared into the outer chamber of the ship, a quick glance told him the pirate had skill. He had righted himself and was coming slowly down, like a man in a dream swimming through thick water.

Pete hit the door three times and then put his weight against it. The wait in the air lock—which he could do nothing about—did not bother him greatly. Unless the pirate's partner appeared from nowhere, Pete was safe.

When the door opened, he found Jane and Rachel Barry waiting for him. He answered the question in their eyes. "I didn't make it. Get down the stairs. We'll lock the safety door and hope they don't get through it for a while."

Safe in the companionway, Pete sat down on the steps and wiped his brow. "I met one of our friends right outside. I was lucky he didn't have a rifle."

Rachel Barry's face bore an expression of exasperation rather than fear. "This nonsense has got to stop. I'm going to call Homer and—"

"Mother! You can't. In the first place, there's a scrambler fouling the channels out there. And I told you—Uncle Homer may be dead."

"That's nonsense too. I know what you told me, but God in his justice wouldn't let Homer die while those two devils escape unharmed!"

"Let's go forward," Pete said. "We've got to find our way into the other section of the ship."

As he spoke, Ellen Barry slid down the railing of the

151

far stairway and came running toward them. She skidded to a halt, her face bright with excitement at this new and wonderful place, her breath coming in gasps.

"Ellen," her mother scolded. "I told you to stay with me. Where have you been?"

Pete, his nerves in less than a serene state, waved a quick hand. "It doesn't matter. We've got those killers on the outside and no water."

"I know where there's water," Ellen announced.

Pete stopped and grabbed the dancing juvenile by the arm. "Where? Where *have* you been, Ellen?"

"Down a hole I found. It was awfully cold. There are big blocks of ice down there."

Pete looked a trifle foolish as he stared at Jane. "Of course! Ice would last for ages. That was probably how they carried their water."

Jane was skeptical. "But the method is outmoded. It's used only on the old tramp freighters."

"This is no time to discuss abstracts," Pete said.

Jane's eyes flashed with a little of the old fire. "What's abstract about a block of ice?"

Pete raised his hands in total frustration. "Ye gods! We're in danger of our lives, and I'm saddled with a bunch of infants!"

"Now, now, children," Rachel Barry chided. "Let's not be unpleasant to each other."

"Ellen," Pete said with exaggerated clarity and patience, "will you show us where that hole is?"

"It's right down there by the other stairway."

The four of them hurried forward, Rachel and her second youngest going on ahead.

Jane fell into step beside Pete. "If you can hold your temper for a few minutes, I've got some good news for you."

"I'm extremely even-tempered at all times," he replied frostily. "And I can certainly use some good news."

"That door at the head of the stairway. I examined it when you were outside. It's made of the same material as the hull, and the only possibility they have of getting through it is by using a light-ray unit. And maybe even not then."

"That helps."

"And I'll bet they haven't got a light-ray with them."

"I'm sure they haven't. But they might find another hatch somewhere. We didn't check the whole ship."

"That's possible. Pete, I think we ought to have a talk about—about things."

"I agree. If things would stop happening so fast."

"We've got to compare notes and work out a plan. If we just sit here—"

"—we're through," Pete finished grimly. "Given a little time, those two have enough experience and determination to get to us."

"If we don't find any weapons . . ."

"Maybe we will."

They'd reached the hole Ellen had told them about. It was in the floor of the companionway close to the far stairway. Her sharp eyes had discovered a circular plate set flush to the metal surface surrounding it. In the wall beside it was a small handle that could have controlled an inside valve. She had turned it, and the lid had uncovered another stairway that spiraled down.

Ellen had already vanished into the lower depths. Pete followed. Above, Rachel Barry called down, "Ellen, have you seen Colleen? I don't want that child running wild over this ship. I told her to stay with me!"

Ellen didn't answer. When Pete got to the lower companionway, she'd already gone aft and was tugging at a door.

"It's in here."

There were no light panels in the hold beyond, but some light sifted in and Pete saw the stacks of ice blocks. He breathed a deep sigh of relief. "So far as we're concerned right now, that ice is the most valuable thing on this ship. Mrs. Barry, there must be a converter unit around somewhere. Why don't you and Ellen look for it? Jane and I will go on ahead and see what we can find farther back.

Rachel Barry's smile was a little drawn, but placid and without apprehension. "That sounds wise. But don't you children get into any trouble."

As they walked away, Pete whispered, "Your mother is—well, *fantastic*."

"She's had to be—to raise us without a father. Maybe she does refuse to face reality at times . . ."

"Maybe she's the one that does face it. We might be the ones who are off the beam."

"It's difficult for Mother to believe anything bad about anyone. It's her great weakness."

"Weakness? I'm beginning to wonder if it isn't a virtue?"

Jane didn't answer because Pete had pulled a door open and they were both peering inside.

"An engine room," Jane said.

"This stuff isn't the same as the memory bank cases, but it still must be under control of the cybernetic brain."

"Of course. The brain controls the ship. But there aren't any moving parts here."

Nor were there any in the next engine room or the next. After they'd looked behind four mysterious doors, Pete stopped and leaned thoughtfully against the wall. "The questions are beginning to pile up," he said.

"A lot faster than the answers."

"Do you remember when we were at the window trying to warn your mother away from the ship?"

"Yes."

"When the ship swung at the monocar, I noticed something. I think you noticed it too."

"I did. Another of those weird, impossible phenomena. The ship moved, but it didn't."

"That's right. I was wondering if our impressions were the same. I got the feeling nothing was moving even when the ship was whipping through space. And I don't care how big or solid this tub is. We should have been thrown off our feet."

"It was as though we were standing still and the rocks were hurtling toward us."

Pete's face reflected a mind wrestling with problems far too big for it. "There are a couple of other things, Jane. One is that we haven't found a sign of any living quarters on this ship."

155

"We haven't covered it all yet. That spiral stairway wasn't more than twelve feet. This level is sandwiched between the lofts upstairs and whatever is down below."

"That's true. But what kind of a ship would have living quarters below and after? At least the officers would be quartered forward and above center. Another thing—the control room was obviously where we found the brain. But there wasn't a chair in the place. I don't think the Captain would stand up all the way across the System."

"The cybernetic brain is the pilot and the captain and everything else, Pete."

"Have you got some definite reason for thinking—?"

Jane's nerves were raw too. She jerked away and appeared close to tears. "I don't need a reason! I'm telling you. You're right. There isn't any crew on this ship! The ship is run by that—that *mind* up there! It's following me all over the ship!"

"It isn't following you, Jane," Pete said gently. "You just keep bumping into the emanations."

"You and your emanations! If you're so smart, why can't you think of a way to get us out of this mess?"

"Getting us out might be up to you."

"Oh? That's just great!"

"You've got to see what you can do with that cybernetic unit!"

"*I* have to! I'm no scientist. I don't know anything about electrophysics!"

"No, but a lot of electrophysicists would give half their education to have what you've got."

"All I've got is a muddled head. Besides, I'm thirsty."

"Then let's go back. Maybe they've got some ice melted by this time."

They went back and found that Rachel Barry had found the unit, but Ellen had figured out how it worked. She was jumping up and down and clapping her hands as a stream of water flowed into the pan.

"Did you see Colleen anywhere?" Rachel asked.

"No," Pete said. "Didn't she turn up?"

"That young one! I don't know what I'm going to do with her!"

Pete had an excellent suggestion. Take the little character over the maternal knee and wallop her good. He did not voice it, however. He was having a hard enough time soothing Jane for the job that lay ahead. He didn't want any more flaring tempers.

"I think we ought to stay together. At any minute we may have a couple of pirates climbing over our frames. We'd better—"

"If you think you're going to find any weapons, you might as well forget it," Jane said flatly.

Pete didn't question her. He was willing to concede that she knew more about the ship by instinct and mental rapport than he could possibly guess.

"All right. Then the thing to do is see if we can find a way to lift this derelict out of here. I guess we'll have to split up regardless. Why don't Mrs. Barry and Ellen try to find Colleen and then check some of that food in the upper holds. These kids are going to have to eat."

There were no objections, so Pete left Rachel and Ellen Barry to search that area and went aloft, Jane going with him without objection.

But when they reached the doorway to the cabin where the brain was housed, she drew back. "I can't go in there yet, Pete."

"But Jane! You've got to."

"I know. Just give me a few more minutes. Let's go back into one of those empty holds until my brain stops rattling."

Pete stopped and faced her and put his hands on her shoulders. "I—well, I don't quite know how to say it, but I want you to know. I've got a lot of admiration for you—for your courage . . ."

Jane smiled. "How about my evil temper? My raspy, hostile disposition?"

"I'm no saint, myself. In fact, I'm not very brave. I'm scared most of the time."

"You'll do, then, till a brave man comes along. Fighting it out here with a family hanging around your neck."

"Actually, I think your mother's great. And I like the kids—"

A shriek reached their ears. It came faintly at first, but it was enough to stiffen them. Gradually it increased in volume as the screamer, obviously on the move, came closer.

"They got in the ship!" Pete exclaimed in horror. "They're chasing one of the girls."

Jane had tensed up, but her look, a puzzled one, questioned that. "It's Colleen. She's terrorized. She wouldn't react that way to an ordinary man."

158

"Unless he shot at her—wounded her!"

Jane turned pale. "Oh, no!"

They had run from the hold and were rushing along the companionway. They reached the stairs as the still-screaming Colleen was climbing them. She threw herself at Jane and clung to her in agony of terror.

"Dead!" she babbled. "Hundreds of them. People just lying there! Then you touch them and they disappear!"

Jane held her small sister close. She stared at Pete in consternation. "What can she be talking about?"

"I don't know, Pete said as he went to one knee and grasped Colleen by the shoulders. "But we'd better find out."

"In there!"

They had partially quieted the hysterical Colleen.
The task was accomplished by Rachel Barry, whom
they had met in the companionway along which she'd
been running in response to the screams. Then Colleen led them to another of the spiral staircases she'd
discovered not far from the one Ellen's sharp eyes had
found. They'd gone down a much longer spiral this
time until Pete knew they were in the heretofore hidden bottom section of the ship.

There, Ellen had pointed to a door she'd left open in her panicky flight. Pete led the way in. But he stopped in the doorway and Jane had to push him on in to make room.

"What *is* it, Pete?" Then she too stopped and stared.

It was a vast, low-ceilinged hold—a dormitory; one in which at least five hundred people were asleep. They lay on low beds set in uniform rows from one end of the dormitory to the other. They lay in various positions of repose, and it would not have been illogical to expect some of them to awaken and sit up and protest the invasion.

Pete walked slowly forward while the others stayed clustered around the entrance. Behind him, he heard Colleen whimper. "They're dead! They're all dead! All the people in here!"

The shock of it hit Pete also, as they stood there, frozen by the macabre, brooding aura of the dormitory. There were some two hundred bodies—men, women, and children who, at some past distant moment, had died there on that ship. There had apparently been no panic. The unfortunates had been sitting, standing, evidently walking about. And death appeared to have come quickly. Gas perhaps, Peter thought. When the brain went wrong, something went wrong in here.

"That was the one I touched," Colleen said as she pointed in dazed terror. "It was—cold!" She buried her face against her mother and clung desperately.

"Yes, dear," Rachel Barry said gently. "But it's over now. There is an explanation, I'm sure." She glanced about and frowned. "It's difficult to breathe in here."

"Let's get out," Pete said. When they were back in the companionway, he closed the door after them. Rachel and the two younger girls looked at him wordlessly for the explanation Rachel had so confidently mentioned. But it was Jane who gave it. She spoke in a quiet, awed monotone.

"They've been dead for a thousand years. They were traveling on this ship and something happened. The air suddenly left the place they're in. It was cut off and they died quickly."

"But they would have struggled," Pete murmured.

Again, Jane would brook no dissension. "That's the way it was. We may never know exactly what killed them, but that was the way it was. Whatever happened damaged the brain at the same time. They lay there dead for centuries while this ship went wherever it went and finally came here, into the Belt and into the Badlands."

"Where were they coming from?" Pete asked. "Where were they supposed to be going?"

"I don't know."

"It doesn't matter right now. The important thing is our survival. It hinges on getting out of here. And I've got an idea about that."

"What is it?"

"I'll talk to those men. We'll give them the ship if they'll let us leave."

"You mean you're afraid?"

Pete was a trifle slow in answering. "Yes."

"No you're not. The Masons were never the kind to run away from a fight. You're worried about us."

"I'm worried about me," Pete said.

"You're about as convincing as a square spaceship, but it doesn't make any difference. You know those men would never let us go. We could make a complaint. That would start an investigation. They don't want one. It would be easier to kill us."

"That's one thing about the Belt that's bad," Pete muttered. "Murder is so easy to get away with."

"Our salvation lies elsewhere," Jane said. "We've got to lift this ship out of here."

"Good idea. But I don't happen to be up on cybernetic brains."

"We'll go to the control cabin. We'll take the brain's lid off. I'll be able to tell you what to do—I hope."

Pete realized what an effort this was on Jane's part, but he didn't highlight the point. "All right. Let's go."

Jane turned to her mother. "You three go back to the escape hatch and keep watch. Stay on the stairs and watch the door. If it starts to heat up, let us know. That will mean they've got a light-ray, and we're in trouble."

Ellen stared innocently. "I thought we were in trouble already."

Jane patted her cheek. "No, dear. We're just on a little picnic. Go with Mother and have fun."

"I wish I could talk to Homer," Rachel Barry said. "I'm sure . . ."

"The only thing we can be sure of is that we've got to get this ship out of here," Pete said. "Let's go."

When they got to the control cabin, Jane stared silently at the cybernetic unit. Her face was empty, expressionless, her eyes vacant, unfocused.

163

Pete waited, then asked a question that sounded silly even in his own ears. "Is it telling you anything?"

"Be quiet."

Pete moved away, around the shining globe. He studied it and learned nothing. To occupy his mind he allowed it to drift to the mystery of the ship itself and to toy with the idea that had been forming behind the preoccupations of the immediate present.

Who were the people of dust? What had they been? What great cosmic adventure had ended here in the Badlands of the Belt? What incredible space operation had been thwarted by the margin for error that lay in simple mechanical breakdown? And all of it had happened a thousand years ago.

"You'll have to leave," Jane said. "Your thoughts keep getting in my way."

Pete walked back around the globe. Jane came within range of his vision and he looked at her with undisguised awe. She had changed. She was still a teen-age kid, but—he searched his mind for words to define the change that had come over her. It was all in her face. Her face had grown up somehow. There were no words. Then he found one.

Jane was beautiful.

"I'll go outside," he said.

He wandered back to the vacant holds and pondered the riddle of a ship without jets; apparently without facilities for cobalt fusion. Nothing less, that Pete was aware of, could move this ship at the speed his overall theory demanded.

He drove the ponderings from his mind. There just

wasn't enough to go on. Not enough data. Not enough knowledge.

One point kept haunting him, however. He remembered the things he'd learned about Barco Village back on Mars. Definite marks of two different races had been found there. The artifacts uncovered indicated a race of normal size—a six-foot average height. But others in a different section of the Village indicated a far smaller race; a people that did not exceed three feet. The logical answer—the smaller one being the children of the larger—did not hold water because of the nature of the artifacts themselves. Exhaustive study practically verified this.

Thus, Pete was shaken by what he'd found in the dormitories below. Apparently the others, their minds clouded by shock, hadn't noticed the thing that caught Pete's eye. The bodies down there were different. There were normal-sized corpses and others that could have been mistaken at first glance for children. But they were not children. They were adults; miniature replicas of the larger ones on the surface, but Pete was sure closer examination would reveal enough differences to make them a different race.

Was this wildest coincidence, or was Pete justified in associating this weird derelict with Barco Village on Mars?

Then, at this point, Pete had no trouble in snapping his mind back to the present because things began happening very fast. He'd been staring out through the hull at nothing in particular, but his eyes had been pointed at the place the pirate's craft had been hurled back to destruction. The scene had been static, but now he caught movement. A figure struggled from the wreck.

Homer Deeds.

Homer, obviously in great pain, had one hand pressed against his side where his ribs had possibly been caved in. The other fist gripped a hand jet and Homer's attention was centered grimly on the derelict. As Pete watched, Homer pushed agonizingly off into space, the hand jet pulling him slowly toward the ship.

What was going on? Where were the other two pirates? Pete ran from the loft toward the lower companionway and got the news from Ellen at the bottom of the stairs.

"Mother sent me to get you! The door is heating up."

"Those men are—"

"They've got a cutter!" Pete cried and ran back along the companionway.

He found Rachel and little Colleen at the foot of the stairs looking up at the door. Rachel greeted him with a calm little smile.

"They're cutting the door away," she said. "When they come in, I'll talk to them."

"You'll do nothing of the kind," Pete retorted.

"Now, Peter, I'm a little older than you are."

"I don't care if you're older than the planets, you're going to take those two kids and run and hide. And the longer you stay hidden, the longer you'll live."

"But Pete . . . a little reason . . ."

"Get going!"

166

Her poise shaken by Pete's almost savage assumption of command, Rachel Barry seized her younger daughters' hands and the three of them hurried forward. There was the impression that perhaps Rachel was in a hurry to get away from Pete more so than from the pirates outside.

Left to himself, Pete put into action a pathetic little plan he'd formulated earlier, not because it was brilliant, but because it was the only thing to do.

There was a ledge above the door the pirates were now cutting away; room up there for one man to crouch and wait—and jump from when the right moment came if it ever did.

That moment would be when the two pirates entered and started down the stairs. If they came one at a time, however, the ruse would add up to nothing; also, if one of them happened to look up and see Pete squatting there.

But even if it worked perfectly, Pete could still kill himself. The stairs were steep and everything down there was hard metal. Still, he had to try.

Getting up on the ledge wasn't the easiest thing Pete had ever done, but he made it and while he sat waiting for the door to crash in he realized he'd forgotten to tell Rachel where Jane was and to get her and take her into hiding also. It was too late to correct this blunder, though, because the light-ray had already cut through and a thin slit was lengthening along one edge of the door. Pete crouched there, wondering what it felt like to break your back—your back and maybe both legs and most of your ribs. The thought wasn't pleasant, and he got rid of it by concentrating on the light unit's efficient work as it went around a corner and began moving across the top of the door. Another corner, then the last one and the light was moving across the bottom.

The door held to the last inch of metal. Then it collapsed; but backward, not forward, and Pete heard the two pirates curse and leap out of the way.

Then a head appeared. "Nobody in sight," the owner of the head announced.

"What did you expect," the other pirate growled, "a welcoming committee? Get on down there."

They came together, neither willing to let the other get a head start. Pete tensed. He thought of Homer Deeds painfully pulling himself to the ship in order to get in on the looting, and jumped.

He tried not to close his eyes, but it was impossible to look at all that metal coming to meet him and his lids were tight shut when he hit the rear one and smashed him down against the one in front.

They'd both heard Pete after it was too late and had partially turned. The rear man had thrown up his hand, the one with the rifle in it, and Pete's shin bone cracked against the steel. This caused the first pain that shot through him. But there were others as the three of them tumbled down the stairway and hit the hard floor of the companionway.

There were mixed roars of pain and protest and, for a few moments, a mad scramble of three tangled bodies.

The forward man fared best. He'd instinctively lunged away from the danger and was almost off the stairway when the plummeting body of the second man caught him across the backs of his ankles and brought him down in a whipping action that slapped his face against the floor. The first blood of the encounter came from his nose.

He came up with a bellow of rage and crawled free while Pete and the rear pirate were still tangled. Pete knew pure terror now, during the split second he put his body back into action. This was a weird moment with time seeming to stand still and his mind as clear as a crystal. Was anything broken? Pain shot through his left arm and he was sure his right hip had been smashed.

But his body moved! All of it! His arms. His legs. From this point on, the pain meant nothing.

The pirate with whom Pete was entangled hadn't fared so well. As Pete came to his feet, the man made a tremendous lunging effort. The result was a grotesque, pawing and writhing of his upper body. Then a squall of terror.

"My legs! They won't move!"

The other pirate had moved down the companionway; clear of interference, he turned. Crouching, alert, sizing up the situation, he flicked a glance at his partner.

"You busted your back," he said callously.

"For God's sake! Help me! Help me, Art!"

The pirate called Art paid him no attention. His eyes centered on the rifle. It had skidded along the floor but in his rush from harm he'd gone past it and now it lay midway between him and where Pete was in the act of leaping forward. Art tensed his muscles and met Pete halfway.

The man outweighed Pete and could have beaten him easily, but instead he competed for possession of the rifle. He sought to wrest it from Pete's desperate grasp but Pete hung on, realizing that in so doing, he hung onto his life.

But the pirate was bigger and stronger with a second more concentrated effort; he jerked the gun away and at the same time hurled Pete backward where Pete lost his balance and fell.

He lay there. It was all over. He had only the satisfaction of knowing he'd fought a good fight. Still, he'd lost the battle. The pirate, not given to ceremony, lifted the rifle.

Then something whizzed past Pete's ear, a bright object that flashed viciously as it sank shaft-deep into Art's chest. Art was surprised, but he probably died without pain. Pete turned and saw Homer Deeds teetering from weakness and pain at the top of the stairs.

"There's only one thing," Jane said. "I don't know what will happen."

Pete had returned to the control cabin. He limped on a wrenched thigh, and a sprained wrist throbbed. But the pain was almost pleasant when he considered his miraculous luck. A lot of bruises, but no bones broken.

He'd given Jane the picture—Rachel in charge back there; the crippled pirate's agony alleviated by the drugs from the medicine kit he'd brought in from the monocar; Homer Deeds also patched up, his condition far less serious. He mentioned Homer's role as a melodramatic hero but left the rest of it for later, other things being more important at the moment. Not the least of these was to reassure Jane that the pressure was off—the crisis ended.

"I'll go out and kill that scrambler and we'll call for help," he'd said.

Jane took the news quite calmy and Pete realized her complete preoccupation with the task she'd set for herself—solving the mystery of the cybernetic brain.

She already had it open. A switch controlled a lifting device that came down through a hole in the ceiling. It gripped the globe and lifted the top half of the shell away, and when Pete re-entered the control cabin he was brought to a flat-footed halt by what lay revealed. The interior of the globe looked like a huge treasure chest. It was a fantastic mass of wires, modules, gauges, stabilizers, and parts Pete could not even begin to identify.

But the most arresting aspect was the materials used. The glitter, the glow, the aura of absolute purity, told of precious stones and metals of fabulous value. Evidently, the science that created this cybernetic brain tolerated only the finest of materials with which to work.

Jane had been studying the complex maze and Pete had watched. Her pattern of operation was strange. She would touch a part and pause as though asking a silent question. Then, as though the answer were in the negative, she would withdraw her hand and place it on another part.

The thing's talking to her, Pete marveled—telling her where it hurts. Then he was ashamed of his own wonder. After all, he'd been the one who'd persuaded Jane that the metaphysical and the higher mental reaches were practical areas for her to move around in.

"I found a book," she said.

"A book? Where?"

"It was in a cabinet up front. It's on the shelf there." She pointed without taking her eyes or her attention off the brain.

Pete went over and picked up the book and began studying it.

"You're getting in my way again," Jane said.

He knew what she meant and moved toward the door. "I'll go outside and look this over." In the door-way, he stopped. "One thing—you said you don't know what will happen. What did you mean?"

"I'll find what's wrong, I think. I'll probably be able to fix it. But I don't know what will happen after-wards."

Pete shrugged. "When you fix the thing, it will work again. That's logical, isn't it?"

"You're getting in the way."

Pete left the cabin and went to his favorite place of seclusion, the first empty loft on that level. He felt that he should go down and help Rachel Barry, but the urge wasn't great enough to overpower his curiosity concerning the book.

It was an interesting object, an example of how comparative but widely separated cultures cleave to the same basic functional principles. It was a book that opened from the left and had a hard binding. But it was different. There were pages inside. The pages were of paper, but the paper too was different. And the symbols—the language in which the symbols were inscribed was the most different thing of all. Pete knew he didn't have a chance of even beginning to comprehend them. But somehow he thrilled at the touch of an object so old he could scarcely conceive of the time span—one that had probably come to him from a distance too great to even contemplate.

For a time he became lost in his sheer inability to understand the writing that he studied.

He was not aware of how long he was lost to the time and the place, but it seemed that he was projected, almost immediately into the weirdest, most unreal experience of his life.

It began with the entrance into the hold of the four Barrys. He noted first that Jane had reverted completely. This, he sensed rather than saw, and the previous Jane—the one he associated with the cybernetic brain—seemed never to have existed.

Another thing about Jane confused him. Her beauty had increased in his eyes. Yet, in this sense, she had not changed. In recollection, he realized that the beauty had been there from the first. How had he been so blind as to miss it?

He knew also, that another surprise was in store for him, but one of a different nature than Colleen's hysteria-heralded discovery down below. This one, whatever it was, had stunned them all to speechlessness, rocked them into something unique—a condition of total dependence upon him. They approached him and stood mute as though waiting for permission to speak.

"How is Uncle Homer?" he asked.

"He will be all right," Rachel said, dully. "That is, he has no pain. And he's very sorry for what he did."

"For saving my life?"

"For what went before. As I told you, Homer is weak."

"I'm willing to forgive him everything."

Ellen spoke up, her voice small and awed and deeply frightened. "We came to tell you something."

"What?"

It was Colleen who broke the restraint that gripped them. "We came to tell you we don't know where we are!" she shrieked, and broke into a torrent of tears.

Pete turned to Jane. "What's she talking about?"

"Look out the port."

Pete turned and saw, not the normal twilight of the Belt illuminating the circular cluster of jagged rocks in the Badlands, but a portful of velvet black glittering with gorgeous stars.

He turned back, confused. "What does this mean? I don't get it. We haven't gone anywhere. But—"

"Yes, we have," Jane said.

"But we were fused to an asteroid. How could we . . . ?"

"I don't know, but we did. I found a series of connections jarred loose in the cybernetic brain. I put them back and the ship wrenched herself loose from the asteroid quite easily."

Pete looked out the port again. He turned back and

spoke doubtfully. "Then everything's all right."

"I'm afraid not. Something else happened. I don't know how or even when. All I know is it had to happen instantly. We aren't in the Badlands any more. We're somewhere else, but I don't know where."

Pete didn't have the least idea what to do, so he laughed and spoke briskly. "I'll go outside and have a look. That makes sense, doesn't it?"

Colleen had fallen silent while Jane spoke. Now she exploded again. "I'm afraid! I want to go home to the *Snapdragon*. And I can't find Omaha, either!"

"Omaha will turn up," Pete assured her cheerfully. "There's an old saying. A cat has nine lives."

"Omaha's only got one—and I'm scared."

They were moving out of the hold and down the ladder to the lower companionway. Rachel was shepherding Colleen while Ellen had thrust her hand into Pete's and walked close beside him. Without thinking, he extended the other hand to Jane and they moved after, a touching picture of togetherness.

"There's nothing to be alarmed about," Pete assured them. "All the problems are solved and the trouble is over. And we're all as rich as Earth industrialists. We can go and live there now if we want to."

Pete was talking to raise their spirits, but those spirits were very heavy and the lifting was difficult.

"That's fine," Jane said with only a shade of the old spark in her voice. "Fine except for one thing. It's dark out there and we don't know where we are."

Pete laughed. "You talk as though we can't travel without headlights. I'll go out and see where we are."

He donned his air equipment, lashed the belt buckle tight and stepped into the air lock. They said nothing as the door closed.

A few moments later he stepped out on the hull of the ship.

His first impression had a double nature: A cold so intense it chilled him to the bone even as he automatically snapped his heat unit to *High,* an emergency level that was almost never used in the Belt. And a black darkness so thick and heavy that it was like a living cloud of pure hostility attempting to devour him.

Cold and dark in combination. And so intense it reached through his body and mind to his very spirit and dragged it down to a level of despair he had never before known.

The despair was akin to panic; enough so that he fought back instinctively. This was ridiculous! Something had happened, sure, but they were still alive and had a solid ship around them and they had defeated their enemies.

But had they?

Jerking sternly at his mind, Pete began scanning the heavens. He knew them well. They had been a major part of his life. The major stars, the flaming suns millions of light years distant. The great sprawling galaxies. The heavens were a great Constant to those who spent their lives in the Belt.

But not these heavens. They had changed to become a new and totally different aspect of infinity.

Pete shivered.

He stayed outside until the living cold had burrowed deep into his bones. Then he went inside.

As he stood in the air lock he made a firm resolution. The truth, of course. They had to know the truth. But not with overtones of doom.

So when he stepped inside and stripped off his gear, he managed a light, casual tone. "As near as I can figure," he said, "we're about four miles this side of Orion."

"But that's ridiculous," Rachel Barry cried. "We must get to a hospital. We have sick people aboard."

That sparked Pete's laugh—made it sound real because it was real. He wanted to snatch Rachel into his arms and kiss her. Strictly out of orbit, perhaps, running against the stream most of the time, maybe, but she was still the solidest human being he'd ever met.

"Jane and I will check the mechanism," he said. "While we're doing it, I suggest you look into the food situation. There are boxes and boxes up forward. See if you can whip up a banquet."

That reminded Colleen. "I'm starved!" she howled, and led the way forward.

Alone in the control room, Pete and Jane faced each other with seriousness but without panic.

"I guess we both know what happened," Pete said.

"Tell me what you think happened," Jane replied.

He shrugged. "One thing is dead certain. We're far out in space—farther than anyone in the System ever dreamed of going. We're far beyond the perimeter of our most advanced science, even theoretical, could possibly take us."

"So there is only one way we could have gotten here," Jane cut in. "Isn't that right?"

179

"Right. We know only the theory."

"The theory?"

"Yes. To exceed the speed of light, which is practically crawling so far as infinite distances are concerned, time and space must be blended or merged into one—become the same thing. That way, the limitations of both are negated. Expressing it another way, to travel infinite distances, space must be bent so that the place we leave and the place we are to arrive at become one and the same. In such a theoretical process the trip would be made in a far shorter time than instantly—in fact, in no time at all because from our point of view there would be no place to go. We would already be there before we started."

"You're making me dizzy."

"Welcome to the club," Pete said dryly, and went on. "What's happened to us, whether we like it or not, corresponds to the practical application of a wild theory. But it happened. We're out here. So we've got to assume that the people who built this ship successfully supplied the principle I outlined."

All fear had vanished from Jane's expression. Her eyes were bright with interest in the new problem.

"I'll bet," she said, "that I hooked those wires up wrong."

"I wouldn't be at all surprised."

"Then the thing to do is to change the wiring."

"Of course. It might pay to be a little careful, though."

"I'm always careful!"

"Of course, but keep in mind that we're not so bad

off at the moment, comparatively speaking. We're only a few hundred million light-years away from our own galaxy. Make the wrong connection, and we might land out where time and space start bending back."

"Is there such a place?"

"I'm not sure, and I hope we never find out." Jane had already pulled the switch that lifted the cap off the brain. Pete said, "One thing first. Before you start tinkering, do you think we could find a radio on this tub? They must have had a way of talking to the folks back home."

"I already found that. Or at least I think it's a radio."

Jane pulled another switch that opened a section of the wall. "The brain can open this panel itself when it wants to send signals. At least it could when it was healthy. Don't ask me who it talks to, though."

Pete studied the mechanism that was revealed. "There are no manuals here—no way to tune by hand. There must be a manual radio somewhere."

"Why must there be?"

"Because that panel up front is for visual operation. The cybernetic unit wouldn't need dials. So the ship is obviously equipped for manual operation; maybe for emergencies or short hauls.

"It's a thought," Jane said pensively.

A few minutes later she found the unit behind another panel. Pete's eyes lit up. "Now we've found something a mere human can understand." He took a position in front of the installation.

"They could have given you a chair," Jane said.

"Maybe they weren't built to sit down. Be quiet now. I have to listen."

"Are you going to call your father?"

"Not yet. I've got another call to make first." He began experimenting with the dials. "Now if these people only paid their radiophone bill . . ."

It took quite a while, many disappointments, and a lot of doubts before a faint, questioning voice came out of the void.

"Who are you? Identify yourself."

"A satellite station in the System," Pete murmured in awe. Then he raised his voice. He gave the operator his Belt call letters and then said, "I'm in a salvaged ship somewhere out in far space—"

"I don't understand."

"Tell him you don't, either," Jane whispered.

"Shut up. Not you, sir. I'm trying to get in touch with a party on Mars—Doctor LeRoy, the Dean of the New Portland Mining College in New Portland on Mars. I don't know the call letters."

"I'll connect you with information," the voice replied.

"This is ridiculous," Jane said.

"No!" Pete called. "This is an emergency. I'm pretty far out and I can't risk losing you. Check the letters and put us through—please!"

There was silence, then some static. Then the voice of Doctor LeRoy, by the miracle of someone's science, still identifiable across X number of light-years.

"Peter? Peter Mason? Why, how are you, son? How are things going?"

"Rather exciting, sir. I've got something to tell you and I hope you won't think I've gone mad, because I haven't. I can't explain it because there isn't time. I might lose this connection at any moment. So please just believe me and wait for explanations if we ever meet again."

"All right, Peter. I'll believe you," LeRoy answered mildly.

"I'm on a strange ship, a derelict. It's run by a cybernetic brain and I think it's the answer to Barco Village."

"I see."

"There are a lot of dead people aboard. I think Barco Village was an experimental pioneering station for a race of people who were much farther advanced thousands of years ago than we are even now."

There was no excitement in Doctor LeRoy's voice when he replied. No unbelief, either. He could have been brightly interested in Pete's solution of a reasonably difficult problem.

"These bodies you found, Peter—were they . . .?"

"Definitely two races, also, men, women, and children," Peter said exultantly. "They fit the indications of the artifacts perfectly."

"Then I think you've hit on something. Congratulations."

"Thank you, sir. It's my theory that the race we're talking about gave up the station after giving it ample time to prove out. For some reason, anyhow, they decided to leave Mars and sent this ship after the colonists. They loaded the balance of their supplies and themselves on the ship and took off. On the way back to wherever it was taking them, it crashed into an asteroid and ended up in the Badlands in the Asteroid Belt. That was where we found it."

"Wonderful," Doctor LeRoy enthused. "Now we'll have actual specimens of the Barco Village races."

"We'll have more than that if we can get back, Doctor. There's something funny about this ship. We tried to fix the cybernetic brain that controls it and made a mistake. The ship didn't even move, but we're millions of light-years out in space right now."

There was the silence of consternation. Then, "Are you sure?"

"As sure as I can be from what I know about star patterns. And I'm pretty good at them."

"I—I don't know what to say."

Pete remembered something. "The last time I saw you, sir, you told me you had a theory on how the Village came to be. Does the discovery of the ship prove or disprove it?"

"I think examination of the bodies will tend to disprove it. I had an idea that Barco Village might have been a prison colony for one of the Outer Planets. It occurred to me that testing the possibilities of colonization and using prisoners as test pieces so to speak, might have gone together. That might have accounted for the primitive conditons we found—primitive that is, when balanced against the sort of colony an advanced civilization might have set up."

"Finding the ship exploded another idea we had," Pete said. "That the civilization collapsed and wasn't able to send for its colonists."

"That's true."

184

"And as to your prison theory, I suppose the presence of women and children does hurt it."

"Another idea I had—that the second, smaller race constituted slaves and servants doesn't speak well for an enlightened civilization."

"Maybe they were just testing the staying power of two different races on their planet."

"That could be. We'll learn more about that later, after checking into the new data. Another interesting field of investigation is open to us now, also. Instantaneous transportation looks pretty obvious. This, you've definitely proven. Yet the ship hit something out in space while apparently on the way home."

"It would seem to me, sir," Pete said, "that whatever happened to fault the home voyage had to happen at the moment of takeoff from the Village. The trip was started or the ship would have remained on Mars. But it was never finished. Therefore, the telescoping of the distance between the planets can obviously be reversed in a microsecond. That microsecond put the ship out in space where it later collided with an asteroid. It must have drifted helplessly, with all on board dead, before that happened."

The intense scientific interest of both Pete and LeRoy, had created a bizarre situation—a calm discussion under the most perilous of circumstances.

This thought hit LeRoy starkly. "Pete! You said you were millions of light-years out in space! And I sit here chattering as though—"

"I sort of forgot the situation for a minute myself, sir."

"Something must be done! I'll have to find a special-

185

ist to put you in touch with. Someone here on Mars—or on Earth—Someone who can advise you—"

Pete started to reply. Then, strangely, he smiled as he turned to look at Jane. There was pride in his eyes, and maybe something more as he said, "No thanks, Doctor. I'll ride with the adviser I've got right here on the ship."

Static cut in sharply, crackling across the voice. Pete waited for a few moments and then turned from the panel. Jane was regarding him with a slanted gaze.

"Did you mean that?"

He grinned. "Don't get any ideas. I was referring to Colleen."

"If I could pick this thing up I'd hit you with it."

"Just try fixing it. Now I'm going to try and get in touch with my Dad."

Jane's lips trembled just slightly. "I wish you'd tell me something."

"What?"

"Where are they going to send the bill for that radiophone call you just made to Mars?"

Catching her lower lip between her teeth, Jane turned quickly back to the cybernetic brain. Pete, emotionally stirred also, put his attention again on the radio panel, switching on the power.

The static was still there, but within a few moments, it faded and Pete sent out his call letters. The faraway voice asking identification came more quickly, this time, and was clearer. He reidentified himself and then asked to be connected with his father in the Asteroid Belt. There was a little more static.

Then his heart jumped into his throat as the raspy voice of Betcha Jones came back to him.

"Betcha! It's me! I mean, it's Pete."

"Great stars! Where are you? We've been waiting for a call. Your Dad's fit to go through the ceiling and take his bed with him!"

"I'm in a little trouble, Betcha. Let me talk to Dad."

Joe Mason's voice was already coming in. "Pete! Pete boy! Where have you been? What have you been doing? You've had us plenty worried."

Pete gulped. "It's a long story, Dad. I hope I can see you again and tell you."

"What do you mean, you *hope*? Are you in some kind of a real jam?"

"I guess you'd call it that. We found a bonanza, Dad. A spaceship. There are millions in the salvage! But—"

"What do you mean, *we*?"

"I've got the Barrys with me. The whole family. We own the salvage together."

"Have you gone crazy, boy?"

"Dad, I've got to talk fast before the static comes in again. I can't explain; I can just state facts. We've got the ship but it's a strange kind—one like nobody ever saw before and we're thousands of light-years away. I—I don't know whether we'll get back or not."

Betcha's rasp cut in again. Pete listened. His jaw dropped. "Are you kidding?"

Betcha's tones became more strident. He wasn't kidding and he resented being accused of it.

Pete laughed with touches of reactionary hysteria in the sound. He held up a defensive hand as though

188

Betcha was there and could actually see it.

"All right! All right. I'll explain later. I've got to cut out now. I'll be seeing you, Dad. And when I do we'll be able to buy the biggest luxury liner ever made, just for you to ride around in!"

Pete snapped the connection and turned on Jane. She came around to face him and he grabbed her into his arms and kissed her.

Rachel Barry entered the cabin at that precise moment and her eyes flashed. "Now stop that, you two! Fine example you're setting for your sisters!"

Jane stared in stunned amazement, overcome by what seemed to Pete's sudden madness. But then he astounded both of them even further by grabbing Rachel and repeating his performance.

"He's gone out of his mind!" Jane cried as her mother struggled in desperation.

"Not exactly," Pete shouted. He looked around at the walls of the cabin. "The plates up here are different. You can't see through them. Come back to the empty hold."

He pushed them ahead of him and herded them along like two amazed sheep. Then he picked up two more sheep on the way—Colleen and Ellen—and shepherded the four of them into the hold.

"I was talking to Betcha," he exulted, "and I told him where we were. He said I was crazy—that he'd just taken a fix on us and he told me where we really were. Look out there. What do you see?"

They rushed to the bulkhead and looked out through four different windows.

"It's light!" Colleen screamed. "I see the sun."

"We're back in the System!" Jane cried.

"We're on Mars!" Pete said. "That ruin you see is Barco Village." He whirled Jane around. "You were changing the connections while I was calling home, weren't you?"

"Yes . . . I . . ."

"And you were wrong again. But it was the luck of space. This must have been the ship's original destination. It was patterned into the brain. It left here for a return to its home port, wherever that is, when it got into trouble. What you did was to rewire it to the original orbit pattern. So the ship brought us back here."

Ellen was on her knees patting the floor. "Oh, you lovely, lovely ship!" she crooned.

Rachel Barry, undisturbed by the miracle, moved briskly toward the door. "Well, I'm glad all this nonsense is straightened out. We can use our headpiece radio units again. I've got to go and call for help. We have injured people aboard, you'll recall. Come, children."

Pete and Jane stood alone in the hold. They were quiet for a few moments. Then Jane sighed. "I'm glad it's over," she said.

"Are you—really?"

"Well, yes and—and no."

It was another new mood. He'd never seen Jane so uncertain, so—he searched for a term—so *feminine*. Or so plain wonderful!

"Things are going to start happening now," he said.

"Yes, I suppose so."

"We've made the scientific find of the century—of the age. Scientists and industrialists will flock in. Research on this ship will open the Infinite to our System."

"Yes, I guess it will," Jane said. There was a certain reluctance in her voice.

"And you'll be of vital importance to them—the things you're in rapport with. I probably won't be seeing much of you from now on. You'll be too busy."

Jane smiled. "As Mother would say, Let's stop this nonsense. There's work to be done."

Obviously happier than she'd been for some time, Jane, after a manner of speaking, took charge.

She hooked her arm firmly through Pete's, and together they hurried toward the lower companionway.

ABOUT THE AUTHOR

LESTER DEL REY is no stranger to readers of science fiction and science fact. Several of his books have received special notice; MAROONED ON MARS won a Boy's Club of America Award, and ROCKETS THROUGH SPACE was honored with the Thomas Alva Edison Award for the best science book in the children's book field in 1960. It was praised by scientists as demonstrating a keen understanding of the problems involved in space travel.

A long series of occupations preceded Mr. Del Rey's highly successful writing career. After graduating from George Washington University in Washington, D.C., he worked at various times as a carpenter, hotel clerk, farmer, photographer, and advertising man. His interests cover as wide a range as have his occupations—from philology, linguistics and history to cooking, cabinet-making and the repairing of old typewriters.

Mr. Del Rey makes his home in New Jersey.